this
One Wild Place

Avril Joy

¶

Published by Linen Press, London 2021
8 Maltings Lodge
Corney Reach Way
London W4 2TT
www.linen-press.com

A CIP catalogue record for this book is available from the British Library.

Cover art: Arcangel
Cover Design: Katie Hall Design
Typeset by Zebedee
Printed and bound by Lightning Source
ISBN 978-1-8380603-6-7

About the Author

Before becoming a full-time writer, Avril Joy worked for twenty-five years in Low Newton women's prison in County Durham. Her short fiction has appeared in literary magazines and anthologies, including Victoria Hislop's, *The Story: Love, Loss & the Lives of Women*. Her work has been listed in competitions including the Bridport, the Manchester Prize for Fiction, the Fish Short Memoir, and the Raymond Carver Prize. In 2012 her story, *Millie and Bird*, won the inaugural Costa Short Story Award. Her novel, *Sometimes a River Song*, published by Linen Press, won the 2017 People's Book Prize for outstanding achievement. Her poetry has appeared both in print and online. In 2019, her poem *Skomm* won the York Literary Festival poetry competition. Avril lives with her partner near Bishop Auckland in County Durham and posts regularly at www.avriljoy.com

Praise for Avril Joy's writing

Sometimes a River Song
An amazing, accomplished, beautifully written book. Masterful storytelling. Gorgeous, captivating, innovative lyrical prose...(we) want to recognise its inspirational content to women all over the world that despite an unfair society one can lift oneself out of misery through the strength and love of the women who fight together for a better life. A magical book that speaks to every sense and to your heart.
– The People's Book Prize

Avril Joy has produced a work of haunting beauty which celebrates the courage and resilience of the human spirit.
– Jenny Gorrod, Dundee Review of the Arts

An amazing, beautiful book with echoes of Eimear McBride. Avril Joy knows how to draw you into the story, right into the soul of the narrator. Aiyana's voice is the voice of the river. I could have gone on listening to that song for ever.
– Kathleen Jones, author of *A Passionate Sisterhood: The Sisters, Wives and Daughters of the Lake Poets*

A tour de force. The narrator's voice sings... I can almost hear the insects and the dip of the oars... original and beautiful... I read it in one great gallop.
– Sharon Griffiths, The Northern Echo, author of *The Accidental Time Traveller*

A great feat of literary imagination...this beautifully written novel will enchant readers, young and old, across the world.

— **Wendy Robertson**, author of *Writing at the Maison Bleue*

Completely stunned by it! The power of Aiyana's voice, the exquisite rendering of the river setting and life around it, the characters – it is incredibly engaging, immersive and moving. And although there are shocking and brutal events, there is beauty and hope in abundance, not to mention love.

— **Isabel Costello, On the Literary Sofa**

Triumphant ...This book, with its hopes for Aiyana being dashed and thwarted so many times along the way, could so easily have fallen at the last, but the conclusion, brought about by Aiyana herself, whose spirit is unbroken, is triumphant. I felt, by the end, that I had been reading an epic tale, not a novel – rhythmic, mystical, poetic.

— **Alison Coles, Book Oxygen**

Going In With Flowers
Poetry is a natural place to express the most intense feelings. But for it to work it has to be more than just expression; it has to be transformational...Avril's poems have that quality. *Skomm* is an absolutely shattering poem and it's not going to leave me.

— **Clare Shaw**

Women in prison are neither seen nor heard, their stories seldom told and even more rarely understood. Avril Joy spent twenty five years teaching in prison and as well as teaching, she listened and tried to understand. She wanted to give the women she'd known a voice so they could be heard. In this selection of scene-setting prose and powerful poetry, she has succeeded brilliantly.

– **Sharon Griffiths, Northern Echo, Eastern Daily Press.**

Avril's work is unsparing but humane, a plea for understanding for those women on the margins of our society who all too often end up in prison, doubly victimised. Buy this book, keep it by your bedside and read it over and over again .

– **Caroline Beck, journalist and gardener**

Listening to Avril Joy yesterday was a treat. She is simply captivating. She also made me cry. Not an easy task with my heart of stone...I've been thinking about Lisa since yesterday. Her words about her have left such an imprint on me.

– **Phil Mews, Author of *Orphan Boys***

The highlight of Durham Book festival 2019 was Writing from Inside. Inspiring readings and stories of prison life from all three writers... I was close to tears at times at the beautiful poetry and emotionally charged stories from the writers involved – a special event.

– **Natalie Crick, poet**

A powerful and absolutely devastating read... The women have become so much more real for me – and I am humbled by the support you gave them both then; and now in this legacy of poetry. I feel that you do them proud – deserving as they surely are of more care, love and understanding than society deigns to give them.

– **Lynne Evans**

Contents

Stories previously published and listed for awards

How the River Breaks Your Heart in *For Book's Sake*, *Weekend Reads* 2016
Longlisted Raymond Carver Prize 2015

Small Town Looks. Shortlisted for Bridport Prize 2014

Crane in Structo Press anthology 2019
Shortlisted Words and Women Competition 2018

White Feather Girl. Shortlisted Historical Writers Association 2017

Flood. Longlisted Historical Writers Association 2018

A Morning Tide. Longlisted Fish Short Memoir Prize 2021

Millie and Bird. In *The Story, Love, Loss and the Lives of Women,100 Short Stories*, Head of Zeus 2013
Winner Costa Short Story Award 2012

Dancing With Mr Benn. Published in pamphlet form
Finalist Granta Garden Memoir competition 2013

What is There to Cry About Today? in *Even Birds Are Chained to the Sky*, Fine
Line Competition anthology 2012

Tokyo Dreaming in Structo Lit Magazine 2012, Newcastle Journal 2014

The Day Leonard Cohen Died

The day Leonard Cohen died, Loretta put on her coat and boots, a woollen hat, scarf and gloves and went out. The hawthorn berries were dark as blood and the earth groaned under the weight of rusted ferns. Below her feet, rivers swelled with underground dreams. She went the high way over the fields, out of the world, under skies like ice, and clouds that didn't seem to know what shape to make now he was gone. She looked for a hint of his loss, a guitar, a tower, a lit candle. She looked for the faces of the women who'd loved him.

She slipped through the gap in the hedge, leaving behind the cries of children hurrying for a school bus and took the fenced path that ran alongside the meadow where clover and yellow rattle had shrunk back to the soil. When the sun came out, she took off her hat and buried it in a pile of leaves under the alder.

At the stile to the open fields that spread across the valley, Loretta discarded her boots and socks and walked barefoot into the blue.

On the long, narrow, path that stretched ahead she took off her coat, unzipped her fleece and flung it at the sheep. An east wind came in from Manhattan or was it Berlin? It was only days since Donald Trump had become president elect and she wept with America. Saw the murder of the future and was shamed.

By the gate to the road, she climbed out of the rest of

her clothes and came back through the village naked. Past the marigolds in their November bloom, under the sycamores where the light crept in. Overhead on the wires, a choir of songbirds sang a drunken requiem. And nobody looked, nobody stared. She was transformed, invisible. Until Martin Parsons, whose family had lived in the cottage next to the vicarage as long as Loretta could remember and who played the organ on Sundays and wouldn't say boo to a goose, came running out with a blanket to guide her home.

'What in God's name are you thinking of Loretta? What's wrong with you? A woman your age, taking your clothes off, and him having to bring you back like that. It's beyond me. You need a doctor, Loretta.' Stephen handed Loretta her dressing gown and a mug of tea.

'I was thinking of going to the Quarry Pool for a swim but I turned back instead.'

'Are you crazy, in this weather? Do you know how deep that water is? It'll be freezing.'

Loretta turned away, she put the mug down on the kitchen counter. With her back to Stephen she said, 'Leonard Cohen died, he's gone.'

'I know, Loretta. I was the one who told you. When you got up this morning,' said Stephen, then under his breath, his back turned as he left the kitchen, he muttered, 'I didn't tell you to go chasing off over the fields, half bloody naked though.' Then turning back, grudgingly. 'I suppose I better go and find your clothes.'

Loretta stood in her dressing gown drinking her tea. She leaned on the counter by the window and looked out at a monster thrush in the birdbath. It sat, puffed up and unmoving. After a while she began to think it might be badly injured until the thrush shuddered, fluttered its feathers, and flew off. She left the window and sat down at the kitchen table. She heard Stephen come back in. He was in the dining room whispering into his mobile. She listened to the distance between them. Then Caro's voice came to her, 'If you don't get lost,' Caro said, 'if you don't surrender, you don't live.'

When Brenda arrived, she put the kettle on. 'How are you feeling, Loretta?' she said.

'I'm all right, I'm fine really,' said Loretta. Her voice sounded small. But it was hard to speak with a howl crouched like a stalking cat, lodged in your chest.

'Really, you don't look it. Look at you.'

Loretta had no desire to pick up a mirror and survey the lines of sixty years or the grey, shoulder-length hair now blown wild by the wind. 'I'll be fine,' she said.

Brenda poured hot water over the tea bags in the two mugs she'd set out. She knew Loretta's kitchen like her own. She added milk. 'Here,' she said, handing Loretta another mug of tea.

'Thanks. Leonard Cohen died,' said Loretta. 'Did you know?'

'I did. I saw it on the news. Stephen mentioned it too.'

There was a pause. Brenda took what sounded to Loretta like a very serious breath although she guessed all breath was serious seeing as without it you were fucked. She said, 'Maybe you should see the doctor, Lor? What do you think? I'll come with you if you like.'

'I don't need a doctor. I just need...'

'What? What do you need?' Brenda clearly thought she was on to something.

'D'you remember that night we stayed out and didn't come home 'til the early hours? When the kids were small. You pulled the car up under the trees, out there, and I said, 'Listen to that, it's the bloody dawn chorus.' The sky was red. It must have been at least four in the morning. Four am. Leonard was always singing about it. Four in the morning. He didn't go to bed at half past ten did he? The birds were singing their hearts out, do you remember? I came in and made coffee. The smell woke Stephen and he came down to see what was going on and...'

'Course I bloody do. Jack went crazy, didn't he, wanted to know where the hell I thought I'd been and what I'd been up to.'

'I don't want this, thanks all the same,' said Loretta, getting up, taking the mug to the sink and pouring the tea away. 'Let's have a glass of wine.'

'Wine? I don't know if there is any, is there? Anyway, maybe wine's not the best idea.'

'Did you ever do acid?' asked Loretta, leaning back against the sink and looking up at the ceiling. 'You know, LSD?' She turned to Brenda who looked confused.

'For God's sake Loretta, what do you want to know that for?'

'Well, did you?'

'No. I never really had the opportunity, and beside I don't think I fancied it. Jesus, you haven't...you're not trying to tell me something are you?'

'No, 'course not.'

'Well, that's a relief. But seriously, you should go to see the doctor, you're not yourself.'

Loretta was inclined to agree. 'Who the hell am I then?'

'You know what I mean.'

Loretta moved away from the sink to the counter by the window. The thrush had not come back. 'Do you know why the sky is blue?' she said.

When Brenda left, Loretta went upstairs and sat at her desk. She slipped a CD into the computer, promising herself as she always did, that one of these days she would sign up to Spotify. Leonard sang of broken nights and mirrored rooms.

Where was her secret life? She turned the volume up, sat back and wondered about the overturning of her soul. When Stephen looked in, he raised his voice over the music and asked her to turn it down. He'd put her clothes in the washing machine, he said, and now he was going to the allotment and maybe for a walk and after that he had logs to order and bills to pay. She nodded.

As Stephen left, he muttered something about wasting power and switched off the light. A small thing. Infinitesimal. A butterfly flapping its wings in Brazil, a tornado in Texas or wherever it was. Loretta saw the coming wave. How could Leonard go and die on her like that, before she was ready? She should have known something bad was going to happen. Should have smelt it in the air. The house was already swollen with winter damp.

It wasn't even that she was Leonard Cohen's biggest fan. She'd never seen him live. She missed the Isle of Wight because her father forbade it and she didn't have the gumption to argue or resist. She vowed one day she would. She would hear him sing, live. She'd held on to that belief, that one day she would resist. Now another November had dawned and Leonard was gone and Loretta wondered how long she could keep up the pretence.

November was always the same. When it came round, everything started to slip away. November, the year nearly gone and what to show for it and how different from all the years of the recent past? Lately, little to show. Years like a slow procession, like the distant echo of bells on a mountain trail. November, axis of seasons, it only took one storm, one downpour and the rusted drying leaves were shed and the barren trees clutched at the sky. Her skin like tinder waiting for the fire. Loretta wondered if she should write it all down, it would be less scattered then. Put the words in a pillowcase, scraps of paper, patches of light through the cracks.

Leonard was eighty-two when he died. Loretta had just turned sixty. When Cohen was sixty he'd declared himself a young man. Loretta didn't feel young anymore. Sometimes she didn't feel at all, other times she couldn't put words to her feelings, though if you pushed her, as Brenda had last Christmas when they'd got drunk at their neighbour Margaret Logan's get-together on Boxing Day, after which she'd been sick on the bathroom floor, and gone to bed in disgrace, she would have said she felt like a sun sliding off the edge of the day, slipping down behind the trees. Something was going down fast, shrinking, dissolving, and it was her life. She couldn't blame Leonard for that. She really only had herself to blame.

But she wasn't letting him off the hook that lightly. No. To begin with there was the small matter of her virginity, lost late, on a moth-strewn, summer night, in a Cambridge house. The window had been open, a guttering candle on its sill, The *Songs of Leonard Cohen*, playing. And Loretta was feeding him tea and oranges that came all the way from China when she should have been concentrating on Michael Soueif, junior doctor, who knew less about female anatomy than he thought, or she'd hoped, but who was kind enough and had a great record collection. Michael Soueif. In the end she had fallen for him and his records like ripe fruit to the dry earth. Despite her mother's protestations at his foreignness, she'd brought him home, brought him wine and bread. They'd slept together, wild-eyed, on a bed of snow under ribbons of rain. She'd loved him perfectly, he'd taught her all he knew. Then without warning he'd killed the lights, ended their engagement and announced his departure. Loretta suspected that what was broken would never be fixed. Her gap years, she supposed that's what you'd call them now, had ended all too quickly as autumn shifted into winter.

Leonard had been there at her alpha. If she wasn't careful her omega would creep up like his and what would she have to show for the years? There was her daughter, Abbie, and the grandchildren, Lila and Dean, who were of an age to be leaving home. She hadn't seen that much of Lila and Dean. They lived in the South, near Brighton. She hadn't minded. She didn't think she was cut out to be a grandmother. If she was, then she would always be thinking about them and envying her friends whose grandchildren were close and she wasn't. But she missed Abbie.

What would Leonard do? More to the point, what would Caro do?

'Leave, get out. Leave the house, Loretta, run in the fields, swim in the Quarry Pool. You know why the sky is blue,' Caro said.

Did she know why the sky was blue? Loretta thought she'd read somewhere that blue was the light that got lost, scattered through molecules of air and water. Blue was a famous raincoat, *the last time we saw you, you looked so much older*, weren't those the words? Blue was distance, stars and sea. Blue was the mussel shell clinging to the breakwater, the old glass medicine bottle, the raised vein. Blue was what once was, what might have been.

'Leave,' Caro urged.

Loretta went into the bedroom, took off her dressing gown, pulled on some pants and joggers, an old sweater and a pair of red, wool socks, and ran downstairs. She put on her coat and her walking boots and made for the front door. It was locked. She went to the back door. Locked. Likewise the French doors into the garden.

'Damn him.'

She hunted around for a set of keys and realised there were none. She had to hand it to him, Stephen was a very effective gaoler. Give me absolute control – dinner at 7pm, heating off at 10.30, shopping Monday, pub Friday, white soap only, nothing fancy, the only living soul capable of stacking the dishwasher and putting out the bins and cleaning the shower tray after use, no creases in collars.

It would have to be the study window. Loretta decided if she was careful she could lower herself onto the conservatory and slip her feet into the wide gutter between the glass roof and the kitchen. From here she could make it onto the old garden table with the mosaic top, most of which had been prised off. The legs were rusted but she calculated it would take her weight.

She opened the window. Cold air stung her face and hands. She looked out at the back gardens across her neighbours' sheds and washing lines, the detritus of their lives spilled out onto the winter grass. And then she lifted her gaze, beyond to the hills. This was where she wanted to be, stepping into the unknown. Where she and Caro had played. Swimming in the fathomless depths of the Quarry Pool.

She held onto the window frame and eased one leg out. She looked below. There was no Martin Parsons waiting with a blanket. She eased the other leg out and balanced her bottom on the dusty sill where the remnants of summer lingered in broken webs and desiccated insects. She lowered herself onto the glass, holding her breath, praying that it wouldn't shatter, thankful that Stephen had insisted on the toughened variety in order to stand the heavy slips of thawing snow that never seemed to come now. She let her feet slide away towards the gutter. Next, the table. Both feet on it. It tilted, wobbled. She could not stop herself from falling.

She landed in a soft, mud patch on the lawn, the patch Stephen was always promising to re-seed but didn't. It reminded her of his hair. Thinning, in need of re-sowing, where once it had been long and lush. Once he'd worn John Lennon glasses and crushed velvet trousers. Yellow t-shirt, footballer's legs, wide smile. Owned a table and a blanket and half a bed. A bed she lay in like a secret in the hollow of the night as she sifted through the ashes of her lost wedding dress.

Loretta pulled herself up to standing, rubbed the mud off her coat. She looked down at her red socks and boots and watched herself walk to the back gate. She slid the bolt across and was out. 'Well done,' Caro whispered.

She hurried through the front garden and out onto the pavement, past the children coming home from school. At the borders of the village, she snuck through the hedge into the clover field and beyond to the alder where she'd buried her hat. Before long, she was up in the high fields. She pulled her coat tight around her to ward off the wind, then veered away onto the path seldom taken. She followed it down to the beck, then up over the old disused railway line. She climbed the stile where a faded paper notice in a child's hand offered a twenty-pound reward for a missing cat. She approached the Quarry Pool from the spoil heap of boulders and rusted machinery. She clambered down to the pool's edge. Dusk was closing in but there was still enough light in the sky that it glittered on the black face of the water. Below, underwater, light was lost. Who could say how deep? Caro had always been the first to jump. Not from this side. No. They jumped from the rocks that loomed like cliffs on the other side. It was forbidden, of course, due to the drowning. A boy had drowned in its dark waters and his spell forever hung over it. What was his name? Was he seven, seventeen? It seemed impossible to remember. Loretta sat down and unlaced her boots. She took off her socks. The cold grass spread beneath her toes.

The breath came heavy behind her. He was out of breath. Loretta turned, tutted impatiently. 'God, I might have known it would be you. Can't you let me get on with things in my own sweet way? Do you have to keep popping up out of nowhere? What are you doing here?'

'Dunno. Something crazy?' said Martin Parsons, as he arrived at Loretta's feet. 'Something absolutely wrong.'

'What?'

'Oh, it's a quote. A song. Seemed to me like you were after doing something wild maybe, something inadvisable even. That water is dangerous. Deep and very cold.'

'A song?' The words played in Loretta's head and a melody drifted in. 'Waiting for a miracle,' she said. 'It's Leonard Cohen, *Waiting for a Miracle*.'

'Indeed, well spotted.' Martin Parsons sat down on the grass next to Loretta. He was careful not to sit too close.

'He's dead. Did you know?'

'I did,' said Martin. He picked up a stone and threw it into the pool.

She heard him sigh, like a flutter of remembrance, the wreath of something past.

'He's dead and I'm never going to get to see him now,' she said. 'I always thought someday I would see him, you know, in concert.' She pulled her knees up close and hugged her legs. Dusk was turning to dark and the first stars hung in the sky.

'I saw him in seventy-six, in Bristol. It was May.'

'Really?' Martin Parsons, the guy Caro always said was a geek and most likely a virgin, had seen Leonard Cohen and she hadn't. How bad could things get? Loretta turned to look at the man sitting next to her. 'What was it, I mean… what was he like?'

'Oh, like Leonard Cohen, you know. Smaller than I thought. Nervous, jittery, but to tell the truth I was more interested in the girl I'd taken, Mariella, that was her name. Of course she was in love with him not me. I paid. And then after, well, she disappeared.'

'Oh, I'm sorry.' Loretta turned away and stared out across the water to the shadowy rocks on the other side.

'No need it was a long time ago. So, you never got to see him?'

'No, not exactly, well no. But Caro did.'

'Caro?'

'Caroline, my sister. Did you know her?'

'I don't think so, does she live around here?'

'No, London. But she grew up here.' Come to think of it, Loretta didn't remember Martin Parsons being around much when they were young.

'Caroline, ah Caroline, I vaguely remember someone of that name. But I was away at school a lot. Does she do something in advertising?'

'Yes, well, she did. Not now. She's dead, like Leonard.'

'Oh, I'm sorry.'

'How can you be? You didn't know her.'

'I'm sorry for you. It must be hard losing a sister.'

'Yes, it is. She died in January, this year.'

'Ah, it's been a hard year,' said Martin, 'for you especially with a loss like that. But a strange year all round. What with all that Brexit nonsense, then Trump, there was Prince too and now… well, who knows what's in store. Uncertainty is the new currency.'

'You're a Prince fan?' asked Loretta.

'Huge,' said Martin with a smile in his voice. 'Can't resist it, *Purple Rain*, on the organ. Fierce. Obviously, only when nobody's listening.'

Loretta pushed her chin into her knees and grinned at the thought of Martin Parsons bashing out Prince when nobody but God could hear. She grinned and then shivered.

'It's getting cold, don't you think?' said Martin. 'And dark. Maybe time to think of heading back.'

Loretta nodded. Heading back sounded like the right thing

to do for now. She put on her socks, laced up her boots and stood up. 'No jumping in today Caro,' she said.

It seemed Loretta had always wanted to be someone else. Her sister, for instance. And who wouldn't want to be Caro? Successful, grabbing every opportunity that came her way, taking everything life could throw at her, taking it on the chin. A woman prepares for her first chemo: camera, notebook, recorder, three Jaffa oranges – always the optimist – and a book of Virginia Woolf's essays. Nothing must be wasted. A journal, notes, photographs, observations, voices, an exhibition, a film, all possibilities.

Not now though. In the end there was no film, no exhibition, Caro was dead. Her voice silenced, but her presence real. She was everywhere. Loretta had only to look up and there she was, Caro looking in on her through the window of the night. Caro, the moon swimming naked in the sky.

Loretta sat at her computer in the moonlight. Stephen was asleep. He'd said nothing when she'd come in, just made their tea for seven o'clock to eat in front of the news. Loretta had declined to watch the news, declined to eat, leaving him to surrendered flesh, ashen hair, buried under the daily dust and rubble of war and a heap of dead children. She'd gone to bed. And now while he was sleeping she was awake.

She waited for the screen to flicker into life, for her screensaver, the image of herself and Caro as children in the garden. It was a still, taken from the old cine film that her father loved to show no matter how scratchy and faded it became. Two children playing in a garden, running in and out of the sprinkler. But even here she is hesitant, standing at the edge of the frame as if in another life, and Caro is running and plunging into the spray, just as she ran and jumped into the Quarry Pool. Caro was never afraid of the deep. She is mouth wide open, squealing, holding her hands high. And then dancing, Caro is dancing in the spray.

Loretta typed in a search for the boy's name. It wasn't hard to find, the headlines, *Boy of Nine Drowns in the Quarry Pool*. His name was Gordon Parsons.

She searched a second time. This time for the house. She'd driven past it last week on her way into town. Small, terraced, nothing much to look at from the outside but near the river and only a five-minute walk to cafes and bars, bookshops, buses, people. Myriad pathways. And nobody to notice your coming or going.

She clicked through the interior photos. It was badly in need of re-painting, plastering in some places. Sparse. The furniture old, what little there was, the bathroom resplendent in avocado green. But all these things mattered little. The rent was affordable. She could see it now, coats of pale paint on its walls, throws and bedspreads, a mirror like the one in the house Leonard shared with Marianne. Candles might burn here, she could see where she might place herself, her books, the small things she would bring with her.

She looked up at Caro but she was hidden behind a bandage of cloud.

An early frost. The morning is cold, but the sun is up. Loretta is out scraping the car windscreen. The crab apples on Margaret Logan's tree, three doors down, are red as the fairy-tale apples in a picture-book. The sky is cobalt.

She's found the keys that Stephen hid overnight. They've lived together too long not to know each other's hiding places. When she finishes scraping the frost away, she opens the door and settles into the driver's seat. She glances back towards the house and it's then she sees Stephen hurrying down the path towards her.

He knocks on the window. 'Loretta, what are you doing? Where are you going? It's only eight thirty.'

Loretta does not reply. She is not about to be stopped. She turns the key in the ignition and the engine starts up. But Stephen opens the car door before she has time to lock it.

'Wherever you're going, I can take you later. I'll come with you. Let's have breakfast first. I've got the coffee on.'

'Coffee? But you don't drink coffee, only tea.'

'No, I know, but you do. I thought I'd make us breakfast, eggs or maybe croissants. I checked, we've got some in the freezer.'

Loretta smiles. 'I'll have it when I get back. I won't be long.'

'But where are you going?'

'Just into town, I've got an appointment.' Stephen looks unconvinced.

'With the doctor,' says Loretta.

'Oh, I see. Right. OK then. You sure you don't want me to come?'

'I'll be fine.'

'I'll put breakfast on hold then, until you get back.'

'Yes, do that. I'm off now, otherwise I'll be late for my appointment.'

Stephen nods. He closes the car door and stands on the pavement. Loretta puts her foot down and pulls away.

The viewing does nothing to change her mind. When she approaches the terrace, its windows and bricks are burning to copper in the newly risen sun. The landlord arrives promptly and unlocks the door. She follows him in. The air is damp. The house smells of mice and old newspapers. Loretta takes a cursory look around. She knows straight away that this the place. She imagines herself at the small table in the kitchen, two chairs and a linen cloth, a bowl of oranges, a vase of hyacinths. She has a glass of wine in her hand. It is warm and Martin Parsons is here and they are listening to Leonard Cohen, or Prince perhaps. She imagines inviting Stephen here and how different that might be.

Outside on the pavement she breathes in the fresh air and looks up at the sky.

Loretta pulls into the lay by, stops the car and steps out. Ahead of her lies the path to the Quarry Pool. Within minutes she is at the barbed wire fence. The fence is deliberately high on this side, to keep people out, to stop boys like Gordon Parsons from drowning. She slips through the gap that has always been there. It is cold here, as if the cold reaches up from the depths, too cold to swim. In the car the temperature had read 4c. Loretta figures it must be below that. She walks down to the slippery, edge of the grey and blue limestone rock and looks down at the water and its skin of ice. She lifts her gaze across to the other side, at the boulders and debris tumbling to the pool's edge, to where she'd sat only yesterday with Martin Parsons. She sees the back of the yellow sign. She knows what it says, what it has always said. *Danger! Deep Water*. But Loretta has been obeying yellow signs all her life.

Nothing moves. In the distance a chain saw whines. She sits down on the wet, silvery rock.

In those days there were always a million ways to get down to the water, through cushions of pale moss, down the grassy spoil heap where stones protruded to offer a foothold, or at the far end, clinging to the low spreading branches, steadying yourself, small steps down, your arms behind you, holding on until you had to let go and grab the next branch. The boys overtaking you, whooping their way down, until you reached the water's edge. Until you stood and looked across the pool to the other side, to the high side where Loretta sits now, where the rock rises up sheer from the water, three or four metres, where there is only one way down and that is to jump.

And when they jumped the cries would rise up, 'Go on, lad. Go on. Go on, Caro. That's it, girl.' But not Loretta. Never, 'Go on, Loretta.'

Loretta doesn't know what jumping into that deep, icy water will feel like. She knows it will take her breath away. It will most likely make her cry out but it won't kill her, surely? Surely not? According to the newspaper report, Gordon's weak heart had contributed to his drowning. Loretta's heart has survived blizzards of ice and not failed, yet.

She hasn't brought a swimsuit or a towel. But there is no one here to see. She looks back towards the lay by. There is no one. No Martin clutching a dog-eared album cover. No Stephen with coffee and croissants.

She waits. Already the sun is melting the ice. Already the ice is shrinking to mere floating circles. A broken reflection emerges. Loretta feels the sun on her back and thinks it is time.

She takes off her boots, then her clothes down to her underwear and folds them carefully into a neat pile and places them behind her. She will not run and jump. No. Loretta will dive, gracefully, like a swallow. As if she were made for it. She will keep her mouth closed so that the water does not flood her lungs.

She stands with her toes curled over the rock, looking down and wondering how she will pull herself back up and out of the water. Overhead a skein of geese wriggles and calls its way across the sky. Loretta looks up. She watches the flight until the geese disappear into the sun. When the silence returns, she looks down again at the Quarry Pool and its floating moons of ice. She takes a last breath, breathing all the air she can into her lungs, then she bends her knees and pushes off from her toes, launching herself into space.

'Go on, Loretta. Go on, girl. Go on,' they shout as she dives. 'Go on, Lor,' they shout as her outstretched arms break the surface, as the shock of the cold and the slap and sting of water burn her skin.'Go on, they shout,' as she tears through the water's mask. As she plunges down. Down, through the deep and into the Quarry's dark heart.

How the River Breaks Your Heart

It was the heat they said. Too much of it was liable to send folks crazy. Too much and the river shrank, and the prairie turned to dust. So it was that summer. It was too hot to move. Mussels popped like firecrackers in the White River mud and dry-landers cast a jealous eye on the houseboats moored in the shade of the Creek.

If it hadn't been for the heat Abe Coker might not have dozed off that morning. He might have fixed his eyes on the river, he might have seen the paddle wheeler as it rounded the Bluff, swinging out to avoid the sandbar grown thick with drought. He might have jerked hard on the rope, and his brother Buck, who was after netting a haul of mussels way down below the river's surface, might have been saved.

Grace Maddox was two days short of nineteen and three weeks short of being Buck's wife when he drowned and her future got sucked down with him into the brown river mud. She was just done putting out fresh water for the hens in their coop on the bank when she saw her mother Ida and her brother Harper walking towards her. She could tell by the way her mother clutched her apron and the way Harper hung his head and trailed behind her that it was trouble. She guessed it was Buck. Mussel catching was a dangerous occupation. She'd gone to watch once – only once, because she couldn't reckon with the way he disappeared when he lowered the weight of the can over his head. It had no eyes and the breathing hose was flimsy as a quilt feather. Going down underwater was near enough to getting your head blown off, he said, until you got used to it that was. But no part of Grace could ever imagine getting used to it.

After they told her, she was blind as Buck in his mussel catcher's helmet, blind as Harper was deaf. Blind to the sunlight through the cottonwoods and the grass, blind to the glint in the snapping turtle's eye, and the smoke from the bush fires. The world carried on without her. When her skin burned in the fierce sun, she paid it no mind. She went about her chores, fetching water from the spring, setting the trotlines with Harper, washing the decks, hoeing the ground, silently, like a shadow in the river mist. So that even Elmer Glass eyeing her from his boat across the river, as he had a fondness for doing, leaning back in his chair, shotgun resting on his knee and his one-eyed dog at his feet, did not disturb her.

Elmer Glass was an outlaw, people said. Done some bad things and come to hide on the river. Hallie Carter didn't credit it. Hallie lived in the boat adjacent to Grace with her husband Lee and their children who Lee beat at least once a week just because he could.

Elmer wasn't all bad, Halle said. He was nothing but a miner come on hard times. Everyone knew how river folk liked to talk and were prone to exaggeration. He'd been a different man, she said, before his wife Carlotta got to wondering what life would be like on dry land. It was five years since Carlotta had gone. And who could blame her what with the mosquitos and the mildew and the way the icicles hung indoors in winter? He was soft on that dog, soft on most all critters, Hallie said. Couldn't help being soft on Grace too what with her being such a beauty and all.

To Grace, Emler Glass was a hungry bob cat waiting to pounce. Hallie's Lee too, for that matter. Not that she told

27

Hallie, but ever since Grace's father had died from a weak heart Lee had been ogling her. Always out on the deck trying to catch her when she was taking a bath in the Creek. Buck had been going to take her away from all of that. Far enough so she wouldn't see Lee, so she wouldn't hear Elmer barking at her like a brown mudcat from across the water, and she wouldn't be reminded of all the times he'd exacted his price from her.

Like the first time. Winter. The hardest time and the water fast freezing, a homeless wind ranging across the prairie and down river. Harper was sick and couldn't trap or hunt and Buck was away with the loggers when Elmer Glass called across to Grace.

He dangled a full stringer of catfish and bream. 'Caught a whole mess of fish today. Come over and get these Missy. People gotta eat don't they? That Ma and brother of yours be mighty hungry I reckon, and you sure as need some flesh on those bones. I'll leave 'em here.' He hung the stringer from a deck post and went inside.

Grace rowed across, tied the boat to the stage plank and stepped up onto Elmer's deck. As she reached to untie the stringer the door opened, Elmer leaned into its frame. Grace dropped her arm to her side. The dog circled round her and sniffed at her feet.

'There now, that didn't take so long. Got me a nice fire roaring if you care to step inside Missy, and a pot of coffee on the stove. You can sit awhile, can't you?'

'I need to get back and fry these up. Harper's sick. We're grateful though, Ma says to tell you an'all.' She reached up for the stringer.

Elmer's hand reached out and clamped down over hers. 'Whoa, not so fast Missy. I reckon that kinda gratitude needs some kinda expression now, don't you? I think a man deserves a proper thank you. Just a little kiss maybe. A kiss

28

for a stringer of fish, some folks'd say cheap at the price.'
He leaned towards her, she smelled his hog breath and the
smoke in his hair and the fish on his cold skin but she let
him kiss her all the same.

Buck had been the one. The one to take her away from
it. They wouldn't stay on the river long, Buck said. Just as
soon as they had the money they'd buy up a plot near
Charles, build a house. There were opportunities on the land.
The worst was over. They'd been saving hard, Buck's wages,
plus the money Grace made from minding animals and
milking, and then the River Tears, the pearls Buck found in
the mussels. Pearls could fetch a good price. Grace had sewn
a cotton bag with a drawstring to keep them in.

'Best sell them,' she told Ida putting the bag of pearls in
her lap. 'They ain't no good to me now Buck's gone, and
we'll be needing a new roof before winter. We can sell the
dress too, buy new chickens and a coat for Harper.'

She'd made the dress with Ida's help, bought the cotton
lawn from the store in Charles, edged it with French lace that
Ida got from somewhere, although she would never say where.
Just that she'd been saving up and if a mother couldn't see
her own daughter right then what was the world coming to.

Ida took the dress, folded it in lining paper, tied it with
ribbon and put it in the box drawer under her bed, where
she dried the herbs and the wild honeysuckle. 'We ain't
selling no dress,' she said. 'One day, one time you can't see
now, you just might be needing it. It ain't for sale.'

The dress was kept and the pearls were sold. Grace did
not argue, she had other things on her mind. Word was that
Abe Coker, Buck's brother, had taken it hard, so hard he
was drinking and threatening to do himself harm. She took
the rowboat and went visiting. It was the first time she'd
seen Abe since Buck's funeral. There was no consoling him.
She tried; she told him to get away from the river before it

broke his heart too, gave him some dollars from the sale of the pearls, said it's what Buck would have wanted and no way would Buck have blamed Abe for what happened that morning. She said it even though in her heart she felt different.

Water lay still and scummy, thick with flies. With each passing week, the river shrank. It was forbidden to walk barefoot in the grass for fear of snakes and everyone was praying for rain except Grace who didn't much care whether it rained or burned.

Grace was hanging a line of washing along the front of the boat with her back to the river when Elmer Glass started up. It was getting to be every day now, as if there was no need to hold back. 'You sure is looking hot and bothered this morning Missy, why don't you come over here. I got me a whole bucket of ice for cooling down.' He laughed and hawked and spat tobacco onto the deck. 'Hear that young brother of Buck's, Abe Coker gone and thrown himself off the Bluff. Least that's what folks at the ice-house are saying. Only place he could find water deep enough.'

Her blood ran cold. Elmer's eyes bored a sinkhole in her back.

'Ain't that a pity now, both of them gone to meet their maker. You ain't got nobody, honey, and that belly of yours all swollen up. Time you started being nice to your uncle Elmer.'

If only she could go inside and get Eugene's gun and blast Elmer Glass right out of the water. Put a stop to him for good. She thought about Abe. She guessed it was true. That was the river for you.

Hallie came out onto her deck; Elmer slunk inside. 'You alright, Grace?'

She nodded.

'I'm sorry,' said Hallie. 'He don't mean it, you know. Want to come over and drink some coffee?'

'Be alright, you see to the children,' said Grace. 'Heard them crying last night.'

Hallie sighed, shook her head. 'I'm gonna leave him, just as soon as I can,' she said. 'He's a pure bastard with that belt and no denying. At least you won't have no man beating your child.' She said nodding at Grace's stomach.

Grace put her hands on her belly. She was waiting to feel the child kick. Ida said it would be anytime soon. Sweat seeped through her cotton dress and she wondered how long she could last in the heat.

It was Harper who wanted to go to the Brush Arbour on Sunday. He said it with his hands. Ida said he was right, that's what Sundays were for. 'Besides,' she said to Grace, 'it'll do you good, take your mind off things. Can't go forgetting the Lord just because it feels like he's forsaken you. It don't work like that.'

They joined the trail of Sunday folk swatting flies, shoes covered in yellow dust as they made their way along the riverbank to hear Preacher Inman preach under the Arbour. It was a mile or so, no more, in a cottonwood clearing, all woven in with vines, branches and leaves to create the shade. Under the canopy you could breathe out and let your skin grow cool as a catfish. Grace sank down onto one of the long wooden benches. It was where she and Buck would have been married, where the child would be baptised.

Harper ran up front to Preacher Inman and crouched on the low stool next to the wooden lectern. The preacher let him sit there and take the Book from him and then hand it back when he needed to read from it. Harper took the Book like he was lifting a nest of pintails out of the plum blossom.

After the preaching and the hymn singing, Grace told Ida she was making her way back. She wasn't hungry. She didn't want a fish fry. She didn't want to hear the music or dance

31

under the Arbour as it grew dark and the lanterns swayed. She didn't want to be reminded of how she got with Buck on just such a night two summers ago.

Grace sat out and watched the quiet river. It was a relief. For once there was no Elmer Glass and no sound from Hallie's or anybody round about, just the gentle plop of fish in the water. The sun had gone down and the fierce heat was draining from the day. She went indoors and fetched a wrap of towel and a cake of lye soap. She walked downstream out of sight of the boats, took off her dress and waded into the river. She floated a while, swam a little, then soaped herself clean.

She heard it just as she stepped out of the water; a low moaning, like an animal in pain, coming from up stream. She stepped out of the river, dried herself and hurried back along the riverbank. The nearer she got the more she knew for sure the moaning and the crying was coming from their boat. The voice was Harper's.

The boat rocked as she leapt up the stage plank and pushed open the door. Harper was on the chair by the stove clutching himself and Ida stood beside him helpless.

'What is it? What's happened?'

'Harper got himself into some trouble,' said Ida holding up her hands as if to say stop there, 'but he's alright. He's gonna be alright, ain't you Harper?' She nudged him.

Harper nodded. He stopped moaning but he was crying still. It was inside, Grace could see him crying inside.

'What kinda trouble?' She stepped forward.

'You may as well know, he took a beating. I was talking to Hallie and he was playing with the children, then they ran off somewhere and Lee went looking. Lee had his belt off in his hand and when Harper saw him coming, well, he kicked him right there in the shins. To stop him, stop him taking the belt to the young uns...' She paused and looked at Harper who was watching her mouth. 'So he took the belt to Harper instead.'

'This right, Harper?' Grace signed.

He nodded.

'Let me see.'

Harper took to whimpering as Ida slowly lifted his blood-stained shirt. His back was a mess of welts and weeping.

'Jesus. Jesus Christ. How can a man do that? Here,' she knelt down and took Harper's hands in hers. He lifted his head, his eyes watched her. 'I'm sorry Harper,' she said. 'I'm so sorry.'

They lay him face down on his bed and washed his back, as gently as they could. Ida put a powder made from goldenseal and willow on the wounds and gave him a sleeping draught.

When Harper was asleep, Grace told Ida to go to bed.

'Don't you go doing something stupid, Grace. Something you're gonna regret. Leave it.'

Grace went to the cupboard by the pump and reached inside for Eugene's hunting gun. 'Go to bed, Ida.'

There was no moon. Grace sat down in the darkness to wait. She knew chances were Lee Carter would be out for a last smoke before bed. Across the river she saw the shadows of Elmer Glass and his one-eyed dog watching and she prayed for once, just this once, he wouldn't call out.

When the door of the boat opened and Lee stepped out onto the deck, Grace stood up. Before he had time to spark a cigarette, she took aim and shot him. A wood duck flew up from the water as Lee dropped to the floor. Grace shot him a second time while he lay slumped on the planks, then went back inside.

Some said it was the heat. Others said a man like Lee Carter had got what was coming to him. River justice, that's what

33

it was. The dry-landers said different, they said the time had come to be done with river justice. Time the river folk got the justice of the De Wit courtroom, same as they did, never mind that Hallie Carter was not after pressing charges and had gone west to live with an aunt who never cared for the river. It was time they said, that the river folk be subject to the rule of law. Folks could not go on taking the law into their own hands, that's what the deputation told Sheriff Hogan Jnr. It was time to act, they said.

Grace heard the motor die in the river, felt the swell of the boat's wake slap against the deck and heard Sheriff Hogan's slow, sorry, boots creaking up the stage plank. She told Ida and Harper to stay sat where they were, then she got up and opened the door. Sheriff Hogan took off his hat as he stepped onto the deck. Across the river, the one-eyed dog barked and Elmer Glass hauled himself up from his chair.

'Hey, there Sheriff,' Elmer called across the river. Sheriff Hogan turned. 'Reckon you got yourself on the wrong side of the river this morning, don't you? That is if you're after catching Lee Carter's killer, which I presume you are. Reckon you're in the wrong place.'

'You reckon so?' the Sheriff called back.

'That's right. I reckon so,' called Elmer. He held up his hunting gun. 'You know how it is Sheriff, a man can get mighty sick of hearing the children crying night after night from the belt.'

'That so?' said the Sheriff.

Elmer nodded. 'Indeed. Now, you go on inside Missy. Ya' hear me,' he shouted. 'Ain't no call for you to be out here, go in with your Ma and the boy.' Grace hesitated. 'Go on now,' Elmer repeated.

She turned and went back into the boat closing the door behind her.

.Elmer put his gun down. 'Get those silver bracelets ready, Sheriff, I'm coming over. Hot damn, bet you never had such an obliging felon, Sheriff, did'ya now?' Elmer stepped forward a pace, rested his hand on the one-eyed dog's head then walked down the stage plank and into his canoe.

Grace heard the motor start up. She listened to it take off, fade, and eventually die away down river. She came out onto the deck and sat alone. Ida and Harper let her be. She sat until dusk when the mosquitos swarmed and the birds grew silent.

When the stars came tumbling out, the one-eyed dog started up his howling and didn't stop. The howl ran across the water. It ricocheted off the Bluff and out over the prairie. It echoed down the White River, through the state of Arkansas, way down to the Mississippi, to the delta and far out to sea.

Grace Maddox got up, walked down the stage plank, lowered herself into Elmer Glass's canoe and began to paddle downstream. She paddled through the dark water, while the world slept and the dog howled. She paddled until moonflowers waned and eagles rose with the sun. Until the howling died away. Until it all faded to nothing.

When the Whales Come Back

The engine is cut. The boat sighs and settles into the water.

'The whales have gone. You're too late, if that's what you were after. End of October at the latest, off the islands, finback, minke, humpback. Now, well there's nothing but the grey if you're lucky and a few old seabirds. Leon, by the way,' the man at the helm puts out his hand. 'Guess you'll be looking for somewhere to stay?'

'That's right,' says Nick looking across at Siobhan. He shakes Leon's outstretched hand, notes the salted, weathered skin, the cracks threaded with engine oil. He'll remember them. He wants to remember everything.

'Can pick up a taxi, just along the waterfront, to the right of the jetty, there. Most likely Sam Fougler, one of the few still hanging about this time of year. Most others are out working on their properties, fishing maybe, depending on the weather but Fougler, he'll be about, lives out on West Chop by the lighthouse there. Find you somewhere. Most places shut up now, of course. Not much call for guests in November. Not many come this way after the fall, not until the spring, April maybe, when the whales come back.'

'Thanks,' says Nick. 'We didn't come for the whales.'

'Thanks, Leon,' Siobhan says, as if saying goodbye to someone she knows.

The jetty is wet with sleet. Nick feels it slip beneath his city shoes. He reaches for her hand.

A solitary taxi waits near the jetty's end. Nick strides

ahead, already his head is bent at the driver's window. He turns to Siobhan and mouths the word 'Fougler,' and beckons. They climb into the back.

'West,' says Nick, 'out of town.' Fougler nods. He glances in his rear-view mirror, catches Siobhan's eye and smiles. He's wearing a navy wool hat pulled down over hair that escapes in strands of grey onto his sweater. His skin is like Leon's.

'You're looking for rooms then?'.

'Rooms, or maybe even a place to rent, for a week,' says Nick.

'My sister's got a place out at Menemsha. Not much more than an old fisherman's shack but it's pretty cosy, got a wood stove. Would need airing. Could soon get you some wood.'

'Sounds perfect,' says Nick.

They follow the shoreline, a flat road bordering dunes and white sand beaches. The houses are solitary and grand, once the homes of wealthy sea captains and merchants, now according to Fougler, home to the summer people with their private beaches. He's been around long enough to have seen them, gave Jack Kennedy Jnr a lift once.

By the time they reach Menemsha, the light is fading. Fougler pulls up on the harbour front, gets out and makes a couple of calls. 'You need anything at the store?' he asks.

'Sure,' says Nick, 'good idea.'

They step from the car and cross the road to the store. While they go in, Fougler stands outside and smokes.

The store has everything they need, basics like bread and milk, coffee, butter and luxuries too – red wine, smoked fish paté and Italian cheese. The woman behind the till seems barely to notice them, just packs the goods up in brown bags and takes their money. When they come out Fougler is loading two bags of logs into the boot.

The house smells of seaweed and wet pine. It has two

small rooms downstairs and a kitchen at the back, the same upstairs with a bath and shower room. Upstairs is cold.

Nick busies himself lighting the stove. In the kitchen Siobhan unpacks the brown paper bags from the store, finds a pan, a packet of coffee and a couple of thick blue mugs. She puts them on a tray with a milk jug and a packet of biscuits and takes them in. 'Is this any good? I can't seem to find a coffee pot,' she says.

'Great. I like my coffee from a pan.'

'Really?'

'Yep, really, reminds me of camping.'

'I suppose this is a bit like camping.'

He looks up at her from where he's bent over the stove. 'Is it OK? You wouldn't rather we'd stayed somewhere else, somewhere like a motel or an inn? We could have stayed in town, not come all this way out here. We don't have to...'

'I don't want to stay in a hotel,' she says. 'I've never liked hotels much. I like camping. When the boys were young, we went camping in the Lake District. France too.'

Siobhan puts the coffee on a low table and helps Nick empty the bags and stack the remainder of the wood in a basket by the stove.

At the window the light is green, the sky cut with black cloud. As the dusk disappears, they sit in the firelight, on the couch, pulled close to the stove, drinking their coffee. After they've eaten, when the fire is low, they go upstairs.

'I knew straight off, the night we met, this was what I wanted,' Nick says. 'Time in some other universe. I told myself, just once. Once would be enough. A lifetime's worth. We don't have to do anything,' he whispers, 'just lie close.'

They stand on either side of the bed, take off their clothes, draw back the quilt and climb in. The unaired sheets are icy to the touch. They wrap themselves around each other to generate heat. He will remember this. He will remember how it felt.

She dreams of water and the skeleton of the blue whale. She is suspended with it, diving from the great roof of the museum, new stars in the ocean.

The rattle of hot water making its way through the pipes wakes her. She can see her breath and from the window a gentle fall of snow. His footsteps are on the stairs.

'Sleep well?' Nick puts the tray down on the floor beside the bed then leans over to kiss her. He seems happy, she thinks, This morning there are no lingering shadows. No hint of what he has endured.

Sam arrives with more wood and Nick goes out to the truck to help unload. Siobhan stands on the veranda and looks back down the bay towards the harbour with its clutter of fishing boats and gulls. Above her a whale of sky hangs low and thick with snow clouds. A cormorant skims the water and disappears into the trees.

When Sam has gone and they're inside again, feeding the stove, Nick says, 'Sam has a car we can rent. I can pick it up tomorrow. It means we'll be able to see more of the island. We can get the ferry across to Nantucket, if the snow's not too heavy. If you want.'

That evening in the kitchen Siobhan toasts bread for the paté, chops mushrooms for a risotto. Nick opens the wine and searches the cupboards for glasses. He stands behind her while she's stirring the rice. She leans into his body like someone who might otherwise drown. Like a woman who laments her man's leaving for sea, who fears she may never see him again, who waits for the sailor's cry blown by the storm and borne on the incoming tide.

They are at the table finishing the meal when Nick says, 'Daniel liked the sea.'

It takes her by surprise.

He looks down into his wine glass. 'And fishing, I remember when he caught his first fish. God was he desperate for that fish, wouldn't go home until he'd caught it...the look on his face. There's a photo. Somewhere.'

'How old was he, when he caught the fish?'

He looks up at her. 'Six, seven maybe. I'm not sure. That's the thing, you're not always sure, Sarah's better at it than me, but even she can't remember it all and then you feel so damn guilty. How could you forget, especially when memories are everything. They're all you have left. The harder you try sometimes, the worse it gets. It's better to leave it be, let him come in the way he does.' He pauses, 'Sorry I wasn't intending to...'

'Don't be sorry. I can't imagine...don't know how you...'

'Cope? By not thinking too much, I guess, especially about myself, I mean. It's me that hurts, not him.'

'Are you angry with him?'

'Yes, I guess I am. Sometimes, anyway. Not knowing makes it hard, confusing more than anything, whether he meant it. We won't ever know. So yes, I get angry but then I think what if it was all just some stupid mistake, unintended. Which is a worse tragedy? I'm not sure...'

'Surely it's worse if he meant it. I mean if he felt that desperate and you didn't know?'

'Then we failed him completely, that's hard to live with, sure, but if it was all a big mistake, and his life was snuffed out for nothing, then that's a kind of madness that goes nowhere. The kind that makes you feel like giving up.'

'You don't though, you don't give up, you are one of the most alive people I know.' Siobhan reaches out and touches Nick's arm. And Sarah? She wants to ask but doesn't. Most of the time Siobhan tries to put Sarah out of her mind as if she doesn't exist. She doesn't want to think about what she's doing to her, by being here.

'Some days I see him everywhere. Some days I almost forget,' says Nick.

'I nearly died once,' Siobhan says, not sure why she comes out with it now. Not sure that she meant to tell him, or that it's relevant, but maybe Nick has had enough of talking about Daniel.

She tells him about the accident, how she was left there on the road, in the dark and cold, how they came back for her hours later. About before, how she was defiant and rebellious, and after, about the long days in hospital, about losing her way. She'd clung on, but no more risks, play it safe. Adrift in her life. 'Everything was different after that. That's when I met...' She doesn't say his name. 'Know what? I have this dream sometimes where I'm under the water, and there's a whale, only it's a skeleton like the one they found in Wexford harbour, we're diving,' she laughs. 'I'm diving with a whale, and it feels OK. Like there might be an ending, like we might go on forever. I can never work out which.'

The snow blows out east and the sky clears. They spend the next day touring the island in the beaten-up blue Chevy hired from Sam, driving to its western edge, to the windswept cliffs of clay. They stop for gas, buy food, talk to strangers, walk hand in hand. The woman at the gas station tells them she was there the day the grey whales were thrown up from the sea and no one knew why, why they'd beached like that, fifty or more, dying in the sun and there was nothing anyone could do.

'They took a whole day to die, poor things. Then they cut them up. A lot of people made a lot of money that day, easier than going to sea, that's for sure. Nantucket's the place if you're interested in whales,' she says.

'Yes. Yes, we're interested in whales,' says Nick.

They cross on the ferry and spend the morning in Nantucket town. At lunchtime they find a café, sit down and order burgers with cheese, fries, salad, Coke and a strawberry shake for Siobhan.

'When we've finished, we could drive up to Sconset,' says Nick. 'It's different up there. Went there when we were kids, in summer, out from the Cape, ate the wild grapes and blueberries when they were still sour, gave us all belly ache. It's probably changed. It was a long time ago.'

'I'd like that. I'd like to see it,' Siobhan says, 'even if it's different.' She means it, she knows this is her only chance, no matter how short-lived, to be somewhere other than the edge of his life. Putting a pin in the map of small things.

'Good because I want to take you there,' he sucks on the fat straw in his outsized Coke. 'They were good times, living on the beach, down in the cranberry bogs and kettle ponds, we were half wild,' he pauses. 'I like that I get to take you there, to these places that were mine. If we were in England now? Where would you take me?'

'I'd take you west. It's where I come from,' she says, 'the tides, salt marshes and cord grass, cockles for tea, long flat roads to nowhere. It's great for cycling, an empty beach, quicksand, a lighthouse on four legs, and the best sand dunes. But I don't live there now, not for a long time.'

'We should get going,' says Nick. As they get up from the table, he stands very still and looks at Siobhan, 'I would go with you, you know, to the empty beaches and dunes, if...'

He sighs into the space between their words.

She reaches out and squeezes his hand. 'I know you would.'

They see it then, unspoken, the path ahead, a grieving the

colour of a winter sea, as inevitable as moth to lamp. There is only this time. The hope of something bigger to drop the anchor in.

'Ready? OK let's go. You never know, we might spot a whale,' Nick says. For a moment he even hopes for it; a whale to lead him back when the time comes. But that would feel like an ending.

Mia Sorella

This is where it begins. Or perhaps not. There is always more than one beginning. But for now it's here. Venice, a November fog, and Liam is standing in the Piazzale Roma about to catch the bus to Mestre. He's going to eat with Isabela, and who knows, if he gets lucky he might end up staying the night. They might drink a bottle of her father's Amorone, smoke the weed he's stashed in his jeans pocket and end up in the narrow, carved bed that creaks under their weight.

This is what Liam is thinking when a woman in a thin coat and a red headscarf comes towards him out of the fog. Her arms are outstretched and she's offering him a bundle wrapped in a grey blanket.

'Per favore, per favore,' she pleads. 'Prendere.' Her eyes are wide. She pushes the bundle at him. 'Prendere.'

She's crazy, it's obvious she's crazy. And she's not Italian, even he can tell. He thinks most likely she's a migrant from one of the nearby camps. He backs away but the woman steps forward. Liam puts his hands out to stop her, is about to say, 'No,' when she bends down and lays the bundle at his feet. Before he can protest, she is gone, sucked back into the fog. At his feet lies a baby.

It's as if no one sees. The fog excuses them. They look fleetingly from him to the baby but they don't stop. A man in a dark overcoat slows but then appears to think better of it, puts his head down and walks on.

Liam picks up the bundle, what else can he do? He can't leave a baby there, unseen on the concrete, about to be crushed underfoot. The blanket is worn and fraying, beneath it is a blue crocheted shawl. He sets off across the Piazzale in search of the red headscarf. She can't have gone far, please God. But the fog is dense and the world veiled and bleached of colour. There are only shadows. Before long, he realises he's getting nowhere. There's no sign of her. It's hopeless. The baby begins to cry.

Liam holds the bundle closer and does his best to shush the crying. He looks around him at the shadowy, oblivious world. Christ, why him? Out of nowhere a woman decides to give away her baby and picks on him. He was just minding his own business, about to get on a bus and now this. Some mad woman lands him with her kid. Now there's no way he can make Isabela's and he'll have to go and find the Carabinieri.

He remembers the office on the Piazzale. He's about to fathom its direction when he thinks of the time he lost his wallet to pickpockets, of how he went there to report it but quickly realised he was wasting his time. He could see it was just too much trouble. He was too much trouble. He didn't belong. The office was peeling and damp. The officer at the desk had seemed indifferent to Liam's plight, the rest hung around gossiping and preening like pimps on a street corner.

It was no place for a baby. He'll hand the baby over, just as soon as he can, but not there. He'll find the right place. Most likely the mother lives in one of the camps in Mirano or Padua and won't be difficult to find. The migrants stick together. She's bound to regret it, then come looking. She'll want her baby back, won't she?

Yes? No? How's he supposed to know? In Liam's world there are no simple answers to questions like this. Perhaps that's why she chose him, perhaps that's how she sniffed him out through the fog. She smelled the guy with the mark on his forehead.

There's nothing for it but to set off back into the city. Liam turns, crosses the Piazzale and heads in the direction of the shallow, glass steps of the Calatrava Bridge. Designed as if to trip you up, they're easily misjudged. He holds the bundle tight and takes more care than usual.

His arms are shaking. Not surprising after what's just happened, after a trick like that. One minute he's thinking about Isabela and her bed, the next it's a nightmare scenario: woman abandons child, gives it up to stranger. How desperate is that, how selfish, how...? He could go on, he knows the script, but what until now has been as shallow and glassy as the steps of the Calatrava Bridge has become stone.

He hurries past the railway station. With the fog and the damp from the canal the cold comes creeping under his padded coat, or maybe it's the shock. But at least he has a coat while the baby has only the worn blanket and crocheted shawl. As he crosses the Campo St Geremia he unzips his coat and with one arm he holds the child against his sweatshirt while with the other he tries to wrap his coat around the bundle. He makes for the café next to the Hostel. If he doesn't sit down and stop shaking they'll both end up in the Cannaregio Canal.

Liam pushes through the glass doors, goes to the bar and orders a double shot of espresso and a grappa. He sits down. There's a woman at the next table with a small white dog curled on her lap. She looks from him to the bundle and back again and smiles. She nods at him encouragingly, he nods back. She peers over at the bundle and says something about the baby looking like its father. He nods again and says he's minding the baby for his sister. The words spill out: *mia sorella*.

The baby sleeps. Liam is grateful. He's not sure what he

46

will do if it starts to cry and everyone stares. But he reassures himself that by the time this happens, he will have handed it over to the authorities. As the coffee and the grappa run in his veins, the shaking stops. Liam lifts the crocheted shawl from the baby's head. She, he thinks it's a she, has a shock of dark hair and the smell of the newly born. She smells the way his sister smelled when they put her in his arms, barely a day old, soft and rose scented. She'd felt too big for him to hold and yet too light. He'd been frightened he'd let go, drop her and she would break. 'Hold tight,' they'd said. 'Hold the baby, Liam.' He swallows the memory, sniffs, and reaches for his grappa.

The baby opens her eyes and looks at him. They are brown not blue, and the blanket is blue not yellow. It's different but it feels the same. She begins to cry and despite Liam's shushing and rocking the cry becomes ever louder and he doesn't know how to stop it. There's only one thing for it, gather up the bundle, pay and leave. On his way out, he smiles at the woman with the dog and does his best not to look like a thief.

The cold shocks them both. The baby quietens. Liam walks back to the Grand Canal and takes the vaporetto to the Rialto. The fog has lifted and darkness is falling. At the pharmacy on the corner he buys a pack of nappies, formula milk, two bottles, sterilising tablets, a soother and baby talc. In five minutes he's unlocked the iron gates to his apartment block, climbed three flights of stairs and let himself in.

It's small, smaller than the apartments of the Venetian solicitors, architects and civil servants whose sons and daughters he teaches. The money he earns along with his savings are not enough to get a decent place, but they keep the wolf from Liam's door and the dealer happy. He flicks on the heating, praying it will work. The boiler fires up. It's his lucky day, or maybe not.

By the time he's fed and changed the baby, the room is warm. He lays her down on the duvet he drags in from the bedroom and in his narrow kitchen he slices bread and makes eggs and coffee and a second bottle that he stands on the counter top. Somewhere back he remembers what a good thing a ready-made bottle can be.

Liam sits down to eat at the table by the window and looks out at the neglected string of his neighbour's washing hanging across the courtyard below. Not much chance of that drying. When he finishes eating, he texts Isabela to say he's sorry for not making it, that something came up.

He sits crossed legged on the floor and opens his tin. He puts papers together, spreads the tobacco and crumbles the bud. The baby gurgles and kicks her legs. He rolls the spliff, inserts the roach and then takes it to the kitchen to smoke. When he finishes, he sits at the table by the window. The washing floats, arms upheld like a waiting child. When the baby begins to cry, Liam picks her up, grabs the duvet and makes for bed.

A sliver of moonlight creeps in through the bedroom window that looks out over a narrow, stagnant canal. He leaves the shutters open, re-arranges the pillows to make a safe place for the baby then climbs in. He pulls the duvet over them and falls into the space between consciousness and sleep where his body is afloat and weightless and his mind drifting wild of connection.

When the baby's crying wakes him, Liam reaches for his phone and checks the time. It's 3 am. The moon is full. A dream lingers. He lost her, then found her in a cupboard and when he opened the door she fell out into a bowl of water and glass. He is trying to pick out the splinters when the crying wakes him. He gets up and takes the baby with him to the kitchen where he warms the bottle.

They sit up in bed in the moonlight. The baby feeds,

milk escapes the corners of her mouth, her eyes fix on him, her long lashes damp with tears, her tiny hand reaches up to touch the bottle. Soon they are both sleepy. Liam imagines himself tomorrow returning to the Piazzale Roma and handing her over to the Carabinieri, giving her up to the hard geometry of guns and uniforms. What do they know of babies and milk, of curves and possibilities, of a limpid sleep washed by old dreams? They can't be trusted.

What does he know, adrift as he is, feeling he has no right to his life, his landscape, his memories? If they'd only kept them together...but everyone wanted the baby.

He wakes in the morning when the doorbell rings, gets out of bed, opens the door and is surprised to see her there.

'Hi, did you forget?' says Isabela as he lets her into the apartment. 'It's the Festa, the Festa della Salute.' She holds out two large takeaway cups. 'Hot chocolate,' she says. From her shoulder bag she lifts fresh croissants, still warm. She walks over to the table, takes her coat off, shakes her hair from her wool hat, goes to sit down but stops when she hears the noise. 'What's that? Is there someone here? It sounds like a baby.' She laughs.

'It is a baby,' says Liam. He doesn't see the point in lying to Isabela, so he tells her about yesterday.

'But you can't, you can't possibly keep her. You should have handed her over straightaway, there at the office, you shouldn't have brought her home like this.'

Liam has fetched the baby. He's kneeling on the floor, the baby lying on the rug. He undoes the tapes at the sides of the nappy, pulls it off then starts to clean and change her. His back is to Isabela. 'No worries I'll be taking her back tomorrow. Do you think I want to keep her or something? Don't be an idiot.'

49

'OK, well why not today then? We'll take her back now and they can start looking for the mother. She won't be far away. She's probably regretting it, she's bound to be, she'll be out of her mind, looking for her right now.'

'Not today,' says Liam. 'It's a holiday. I didn't forget as it happens. Probably no-one there. Besides I promised myself I'd go to the Festa like a real Venetian. Coming?'

'But what about the baby?'

'It's cool. We'll take her with us. You don't think I'd just leave her here alone do you? Watch her while I take a shower, will you? I won't be long.'

Outside the day is made for a festival. The sun shines in a winter blue sky, glittering off the rooftops and cupolas, crystalline on the water. They join the crowds, crossing the Grand Canal on the newly erected pontoon bridge. Liam has the baby strapped to him in a sling that Isabela helped him make from a flat cushion and a sheet. He's wearing his old second-hand coat, not the padded one, but the long, blue overcoat that makes him feel like someone else. It's buttoned around the baby. His arms are shoring her up. She seems content. Safe, for now. For now, they are like any family shuffling their way through the crowds to the Basilica.

Isabela buys two candles from the stallholders outside and they file up the steps and enter to make their pilgrimage. To give their centuries-old thanks, like true Venetians, for the end of the plague that ravaged the city.

The sheer mass of people, the baby's head turned to his chest, the flickering candles, the lustre of Istrian stone and polished plaster all contribute to a high that Liam hasn't felt since way back. Since he was ten maybe and he snorted his first line of coke with the big boys.

When they've given up their candles and are back outside, they walk along the Zaterre in a world made of shimmering reflections. Liam stops to look across at the churches of Giudecca hovering weightless above the water on the far side of the lagoon. He turns to Isabela who's looking at her phone. He's light-headed, he needs food, wants lunch, something substantial before they go back. He's thinking lunch followed by bed.

But Isabela says, 'Sorry, I've got to get back, pack my things. I'm going away remember? Taking my mother to see my uncle in Naples. He's sick. You haven't forgotten, have you? You'll cover the students, you have the addresses.'

Liam nods, 'Sure.'

'I'll see you when I get back – by which time no bambino, hey?'

'No, course not,' says Liam.

'Why you keep this baby?' Asks Allegra. Allegra lives in the apartment below Liam. She speaks English. She worked for a while in London. He bumps into her at the bottom of the stairs. He's been trying to avoid her.

'She's my sister's,' he says, then adds, 'my niece.'

'Your sister, the baby is your sister?'

'That's right,' says Liam. He's not in the mood for correcting her English or anyone else's and that includes the lycée students and the groups he's supposed to be covering for Isabela. Isabela's been gone four days. Liam has not been to work and he's given up answering calls and texts.

'Babies are not allowed,' says Allegra. 'I hear her crying. If the landlord find out he will make you to go.'

'That's OK, she won't be here long. Not long now,' says Liam. 'Excuse me but I've got an appointment.' He smiles and readjusts the baby-carrier he bought to replace the curtain.

'She is very beautiful,' says Allegra, touching the baby's hand.

Liam can't get away quick enough. He doesn't settle until he's out of the building, streets away, away from Allegra's eyes.

Liam has a new routine. After the first few sleepless nights, he's sorted everything. No more crying. Each morning he gets the baby up and ready and then takes off with the baby strapped to his chest. He wanders the calles, perpetually lost but content, lured this way and that by a sudden vista, by myriad possibilities. Together they frequent the small, hidden squares and gardens of the city, its waterways and its vaporous churches. The baby cries less, lulled by the warmth of Liam's body and by bottles of tea.

She smiles at him now. He's sure of it. She sees him. He sees through her to the torn sofa, its stuffing hanging loose, her lying precarious and prone in his arms.

'Don't drop, be careful, don't drop the baby, Liam,' they said. 'Hold tight. Look after her.'

The suitcase is packed. It is bigger than him. It stands beside the leaking sofa, the yellow blanket ready. He is digging his feet into the thin carpet.

On the sixth day, Liam takes the ferry across to the islands to the Lido where he walks down its central boulevard to the sea. He stands on the beach under a pale winter sun along with the fisherman. He stands at the edge of the Adriatic watching it roll in, dreaming his sea dreams, dreams of a watery, undercover life. Babies can swim, he's seen it on TV. They are born swimmers. All you have to do is throw them into the water and they'll swim. It's instinct. They don't drown. Liam didn't learn to swim. But now perhaps he thinks he can, after all, perhaps he is like the baby. He is a swimmer. Together they cannot drown.

'You need someone to mind the baby?' asks Allegra. This

time she catches him in the narrow calle outside their building. 'When you go to work, eh? I can help.'

'No thanks. I'm on holiday,' says Liam.

Allegra looks at the baby whose eyes are closed. 'She is sleeping again? The landlord is coming soon, I think.'

'Cool,' says Liam and goes back up the stairs to the apartment and bolts the door. He calls his dealer then switches off his phone. The siren sounds for the aqua alta. They stay inside while the city swells around them, its pavements encrusted with salt and lapped with seaweed. They watch from the window. Her face has become his familiar. She is weightless. They are mute, inseparable.

He's heard nothing from Allegra or the landlord. Who cares anyway? He's not going to make the same mistake twice is he? That's why he'd come here, why he'd stayed, and he was right, wasn't he? He knew this place. Something persuaded him that she was here. In the end, his sister would appear like a ghost on the sands of the sea, on the wave of winter, at the vaporetto stop, disappearing down a narrow calle, sipping hot chocolate in a café frequented only by Venetians, her face reflected in glass. And he would know her. That's what made him stay. And he's not about to give her up.

The day before Isabela is due back Liam goes out early, the baby strapped to him. The wind bites. The sky is the colour of ash. He stops in a small café by the gondola boatyard. The windows are steamy. It will be warm there and he needs something to eat. He steps inside, orders a glass of red wine and sits down. The baby stirs but makes no sound. An old man sitting on the bench beside him, asks after her.

'Mia sorella,' says Liam.

The old man sips his coffee and tells Liam she reminds

him of his grandson. 'He was the first, our first grandchild, but his chest it wasn't good. He suffered from the asthma and then the winter came, his first winter and he was taken. Without warning. This city, damn it, it's cursed, too damp for anything bar the rats and the rich.'

Liam says he's sorry.

The old man says his daughter is expecting another child and she is thinking, they are thinking, of leaving.

Outside, the wind is chill and the ground under Liam's feet is cold and wet. It's true the city is drowning. It's no place for a baby. The soles of his trainers have worn thin. He's been here before. Every city he visits, sooner or later turns its back on him.

In the Piazzale Roma, the crowds are thinning. Liam looks at his phone and reads the last message from Isabela. She will see him tomorrow, she hopes work has been OK. She hopes the baby is back with her mother. He deletes the message, walks over to the litter bin and dumps the phone.

When the bus pulls in, Liam climbs aboard with the bundle and settles into his seat. The bus starts up and the throb of the engine bites at the soles of his feet. As they pull away, Liam leans his head against the window and waits for the bridge, for the water and the play of light on the dark lagoon.

The bus stops in the central square and Liam gets off. He makes for the café across the street where he orders coffee and asks if they will warm a bottle. They smile at him indulgently, take the bottle and tell him to sit. Liam has learned how sympathetic people are to a young man alone with a child. He sits down by the window and watches the square. They bring the bottle and coffee to his table.

It isn't long before he sees a group of men he guesses must be from the camp. They're gathering in the opposite corner, under an Aleppo pine and sharing a cigarette. They're dressed in worn jeans, shabby puffer jackets and wool hats. He can follow them he thinks, this way he will get to the camp without asking or arousing suspicion.

He has already dreamt a past: parents buried in the rubble, a long journey on foot and by sea, a suitcase and a yellow blanket lost, most likely stolen and with them his passport. It could all make sense. He would not be the only brother alone with a sister, in search of home. But who knows what waits in the camp? Fate has given him a sister. Fate has taken a sister away. Liam gets up from the window seat, pays for his coffee and leaves the café. He pushes through the glass doors and hurries out across the square towards the Aleppo pine.

Small Town Looks

She was trouble, my sister, right from the word go. Right
from the world of the womb where she kicked and shoved
and shouldered our poor mother's belly until she swore it
had taken a beating. Right from the skinny schoolgirl who
followed us boys everywhere so that we had to invent a
world of lies and must-dos and can't-haves to evade her. She
was trouble alright, what with her black hair, eyes as big as
sand pools and dark as the night tide. Film star looks and
didn't she know it. Looks that were just too big for a small
town in 1963. Looks that trapped her like the bee in the
honey jar.

And here she is, Enid. Look at her now spreading out the
picnic blanket under the flickering trees, full-skirted, small-
waisted, wide belt, in that Dior dress she made, all cotton
flower and lollipop swirls. If she's good at anything, if Enid
loves anything, it's clothes and making them.

She's the spit of Elizabeth Taylor but Arnie her husband,
poor bloke he's no Richard Burton, doesn't have that kind
of substance, that passion in him, and she needs that spilling-
over adoring, fighting passion because she knows she can
call it up. It's her God given, and though it doesn't seem
right for a brother to say it or think it, she deserves it.

I'd warned her, like a good brother should, told her people
were talking. Her place was at home looking after Arnie
and the kids. They're nice kids too, because she's got style,
she's bringing them up smart, makes all their clothes. Enid's

kids are going to be somebody, someday. You've got to hand it to her in that respect, they may have missed out on that love thing that some mothers do, but they're going places.

Enid might not be hot on motherly love, but just look at the picnic she's laying out in the Tupperware boxes: homemade crimped pasties, cucumber sandwiches, miniature éclairs, Victoria sponge. And now she's kicking her shoes off, walking across the flutter shadowed, sun spangled grass to the stream, dangling a bottle of elderflower wine in one hand and lemonade in the other.

The whole family are here: our parents, Eileen and Jack, my brothers, Billy and his new wife Pearl, Mikey and his latest girlfriend Mary-Anne whose father owns a shiny haulage company in town, bought outright with the black money he made in the war. Then there's me, Freddie, after Fred Astaire, married to Jean who isn't here because she's working a late shift at the hospital.

We'd started to make a thing of it, Sunday drives out, a picnic in some beauty spot, like the combe: stream running through, yellow dressed flag iris, paddling stones silky smooth under your toes. The kids building dams and fishing for brown minnows and speckled newts. Only today is different. Not the place with its narrow flinty track that opens like a woman, a grassy cleft in the hills, flat low banked stream you can just step into, spring water that turns your feet to ice. No, the combe is the same. It's the people who are different and that's where the trouble lies.

I'd seen it coming a mile off, this thing with Enid and Marcus. God knows what Arnie sees or what he's thinking stretched out on the picnic blanket head stuck in the News of the World. Maybe that's it, maybe his chosen path is avoidance. Or maybe he just can't keep up with a wife like Enid, because Enid's something to keep up with all right.

Who invited Marcus and Diane? And where did he come

by a name like that? You've only got to look at him to see he's all flight and shift. Marcus Box, estate agent. I've seen alright, the way he looks at Enid and the way when he's around she's like a woman in front of a camera. Why does no one else see?

Billy and Pearl are off building dams with the kids, letting their feet turn to stone. Mikey and Mary-Anne are already out of the combe and into the alder woods. Mother and Father are sitting on their canvas picnic chairs brewing up on the calor gas, silent as ever.

Diane, Marcus's wife is a pale thing, like a piece of wet washing strung on the line. She's lying on her side on the tartan rug with her back to Marcus, her freckled legs hunched up. Why doesn't she turn and look? And why is Arnie always asleep even when he's meant to be reading the newspaper?

'Smoke?' says Marcus holding out a packet of Park Drive.

'No thanks,' I say.

'Don't mind if I do,' says Enid. She takes one, curls her legs under her and leans forward to catch the lighter he's already flicked into action for her. She tilts her head back, draws on the cig and pats her hair. She reaches into a straw bag and pulls out a couple of Pale Ales and rolls one across the grass first to me, then to Marcus.

'What about Arnie's beer?' I say.

'There's one for him, if he ever wakes up.' I catch the look then.

Marcus fetches the wine from the stream and pours her a glass. Enid's drinking from the glass and looking over the top at him. The kids are back demanding lemonade and crisps. Billy and Pearl are back, complaining about the icy water and drying their feet. There's no sign of Mikey and Mary-Anne. Billy's rolling his trousers back down and putting his socks on. Mother offers him tea and a sausage roll. Enid shoos the kids off with double rations of chocolate and crisps.

Three cigarettes down plus beer and wine and Marcus is standing up and reaching his arm out pulling Enid to her feet. 'Come on then, if you want to find the spring, probably miles away through all that heather.'

Enid's giggling, doesn't take much to get her tipsy, never did. Arnie's snoring but Diane rolls over, 'Where you two going?' She asks.

'Find the spring,' says Marcus, 'Coming?'

Mother looks up, exchanges glances with Billy and Pearl, she's no fool, not where Enid's concerned. None of us are.

'I don't think so,' says Diane.

Enid's brushing down the skirt of her dress. Her hand is resting on Marcus's arm. 'In these shoes?' she says like butter wouldn't melt. She puts out a leg, turns it to show a thin kitten heel and a bow.

'Borrow mine,' says Diane.

She must be crazy if she can't see. Maybe she can and she wants rid of him, Marcus with his ferrety eyes and his thick mouth. Maybe she's sick of watching the shadows flicker on the walls while he sweats over her. Why haven't they got any children?

What is it with us lot, is Enid the only one? 'Only has to look at me and I'm up the bloody spout.' She was looking in the mirror when she said it. I was home from National Service on my last leave, lying full stretch on the sofa wondering if I'd ever look as good without the uniform and whether Jean had twigged about me and Maisie. I was thinking maybe it was time to call it a day and time to fix myself up with a job.

That's the other thing about Enid, where the trouble hangs out, where its spores are cast, where they puff up and burst into the air around her: one minute she's all class and Vogue patterns and white gloves and the next she's mouthing off with the brickies on the site, sitting down with them in their tin hut, flashing suntanned nylons, more than that even, crude as you like, at tea break while I'm in the office.

She's swapped shoes with Diane, put the lids on her picnic food and pulled her sunglasses down, 'Won't be long.' She gives me a look that says, don't. Don't stop my fun. You forget, we're two of a kind. It was the same look she gave me the day she was seventeen and the police brought her home. Picked her up shoplifting a bottle of *Evening in Paris*. 'Evening in the bloody nick is what she needs,' father said. In the end it was only me who could calm him down. I was always the one she turned to.

Enid and Marcus are gone now, nearly out of sight past the other picnickers, the spread blankets and the Hillmans and the Austins, into the wood. I know that wood, it's dark in there, tree shadowy, musty dark, there's a stagnant mouldy pool where frogs croak under stones and ferns, but if you walk far enough you reach the steep path up into the purple heather of the moor where you can find the spring and lie hidden in the hum of hungry bees.

I help the kids, they're ambitious now, making a pool to fill with the fish they've yet to catch. Before long other kids join them. It's instant friendship, the kind only kids do and I'm grateful to get out of the stream and warm my feet.

I lie in the sun. Dad passes me his paper. I take a quick squint at the football results but I can't settle and neither can Mother, whose head and eyes I see turning in the direction of the woods and then raising up to the tops of the moor.

When Mikey and Mary-Anne come back we play rummy. They haven't seen Enid and Marcus. The kids join in, then declare they're hungry. Everyone is hungry. I look at my watch. Arnie's woken up. 'They're a while then,' he says to me, 'how long ago did you say they went? How far is that bloody spring?'

'An hour at least to get there,' I say, exaggerating.

'That far! Better start this lot then, I'm bloody ravenous.' He prises off the Tupperware lids and starts on Enid's picnic.

Diane picks lettuce from the fringes of a bridge roll and swats away a wasp. Everyone is eating but I'm not hungry. I drink another beer, lie back and smoke. It's quiet for a bit, just the sound of people shifting out of the midday heat into the shade, other families at their picnics, kids calling in the stream.

Arnie stuffs two éclairs in his mouth, wipes the cream from his lips with the back of his hand and declares that he's finished eating, and that as Enid and Marcus aren't back, and as they've been gone over an hour, he's going to look for them.

'I'll come with you,' says Diane.

'In this heat?' I say, sitting up, 'why not give it another fifteen minutes and then if there's no sign of them I'll go? Need to stretch my legs but they'll be back before then anyway.'

'Have your tea first, son.' Father hands Arnie a mug of tea.

'Sugar, Arnie?' asks Mother, holding out an open box of Tate and Lyle cubes, which she saves for special occasions. 'What about you Diane? Tea?'

Diane shakes her head then puts her hand up to shade her eyes and looks towards the wood and beyond to the moor. She stands up. 'I'll go,' she says then looks down at her bare feet and Enid's kitten heels lying on the edge of the blanket.

'No need, look isn't this them?' I squint into the sun, swallow hard, my throat constricts as I will the dark figure emerging from the wood to be Marcus. We strain our necks and eyes. I'm praying now, let it be him, and sure enough it is. It's Marcus, and Enid a step or so behind.

'You took you time,' says Arnie, when they reach the blanket. He looks his wife up and down.

'It's a long bloody way to the top and back,' says Enid. She's still wearing her sunglasses, her face is red from the sun, she smoothes the skirt of her dress under her and flops down on the blanket facing Arnie with her back to me. 'Where's the lemonade?'

Marcus is complaining of the heat and the bees, 'Got bloody stung didn't I. Full of the buggers up there.' He's rolling up his shirt sleeve, showing everyone the angry patch of red on his forearm. He goes over to the stream, kneels and splashes water at his face and his sting.

The kids run over to Enid, 'Did you find the spring? Did you get that far?'

Arnie mutters under his breath, 'All the fucking way if you ask me.' He looks at me and I know it's coming. I'm looking at the scrap of purple heather caught in Enid's hair and I'm waiting for it to start.

'Right. Home now,' says Arnie and he calls the kids over. When he tells them they're going they start protesting and asking why, so I say, 'You go on. I'll bring them back later.' Enid doesn't argue. As she stands up I follow the ladder in her suntanned nylons right up to the grass and heather stained lollipop swirls on her skirt.

We're among the last picnickers to leave. I reckon, let the kids play, let Arnie and Enid sort things out. Marcus and Diane have gone. Mikey and Mary-Anne too. Billy and Pearl take mother and father with them. I'm hoping things will be sorted by the time I get back with the kids. No such luck.

When we turn the corner into West Avenue, Enid is sitting outside number three, on the lawn, her head down, surrounded by her life: shoes, clothes, handbags, scarves, hairspray, perfume, that black straw hat she wore to our wedding, the mohair suit she made, her wedding veil, tangled spools of cotton, tape measures, scissors, pieces of cloth and her sewing machine which is in pieces. She looks up when I stop the car but she doesn't move.

I take the children inside. Arnie's watching a cowboy on TV. 'Bed,' he says and they don't need a second telling. They disappear. 'She's not coming back in here, I don't care what you say,' says Arnie.

I figure it's not worth arguing. Arnie'll get over it, he'll relent, just wants to assert himself for once and maybe that's a good thing, maybe it's what she needs. Her wings clipping.

Enid's hair is flattened on one side and her face is swollen, a bruise has formed across her cheekbone dark as her eyes. Together we gather her things up and put them in the boot of my car. We leave the sewing machine, it's past saving.

'Did he hit you?' I say.

She nods.

'Well, you bloody deserve it, going off like that, what were you thinking of? Who do you think you are? This isn't bloody Hollywood Enid, you can't go getting yourself all dolled up running round with other men.' I look at her next to me in the car. Enid never cries but she looks like she's going to cry now, so I say, 'Come on let's go home,' and I reach over and squeeze her hand.

When Jean gets back from the hospital it's close to midnight and she's got her work-weary, mithering face on. Enid's asleep in the spare room. I tell Jean what's happened.

'Well she's not staying here, not the way she carries on. No way. She'll have to go in the morning. She should go back and look after her kids like a proper mother.'

'Have you forgotten?' I say.

'Forgotten what?' She turns away from me.

'You know fine well what she did for you, for us, when we lost the baby. If it hadn't been for Enid...'

63

'This is different. The way she's behaving, it's not right.'

'Who says?'

'The world, the whole bloody town, everyone, everyone knows it's not the way a married woman should behave.'

'Do they? Well so bloody what?' I say.

'She's trouble, your sister, always has been. She wants to grow up.'

'She's twenty-six for God's sake, and they wouldn't be saying it if she was a bloke, would they? Wouldn't give a monkey's. She staying and that's it.'

In the morning when I get up for work, Enid's there in the kitchen drinking coffee. Jean's still sleeping or at least pretending to sleep.

'Thanks for yesterday,' Enid says. She's leaning against the sink with her back to the window. Her eyes look past me. 'Sorry about the trouble. I'll make you breakfast before I go if you like.'

'You don't have to go, you can stay, stay as long as you like,' I say.

'No, I should get back for the children.'

'But Arnie...'

'I'll sort it, smooth it all over, you'll see. No more rows.' She puts her mug down on the sink side and comes over and hugs me and I hug her because she might be trouble but she's my sister. 'I'll come by later after work, bring your stuff, make sure you're OK.'

'OK.' She smiles. 'We found the spring,' she says looking up at me. She smiles again. She's got a different dress on, girlish, A line, pale cotton. She's done something with her hair, flicked it up and out at the ends, and the sun is catching her thin, bare arms. That's how I like to remember her, all Jackie Kennedy and sunlight. I try not to think of the heather caught in her hair. I try not to think of the bees or the picnic or of looking for the spring. I try not to remember going to hers after work, or to the hospital, or seeing Arnie and the kids all broken down like that. I remember her as she was that morning and I think all of us, we should have done more.

Crane

Back then, she lived on Chinese takeaways, cheese on toast and tinned soup. She was an opportunistic feeder from the start. But she did not eat worms or snails or small crustaceans. Not then. Then she smelt of salt and lavender, not bones and fish.

He fell in love with her at first sight, which was something he didn't believe in. In one fell swoop she took all the science from him and crumpled it like waste-paper in the bin. One day he was a man who'd bought his first house and set up home with wife and child, a man with a decent job at the university, a project he cared about. The next he was ready to risk everything.

She'd come with the eggs taken from the cranes' nests deep in the swamp, driving across the German Dutch border in the department's van.

'The cranes cry for two days when they see their eggs are gone,' she told him. 'But we are careful to steal only once, from each pair.'

When she stepped from the van, bird-like, feather-boned, and threw her head back shaking her dark hair, he could not take his eyes off her.

She spoke English surprisingly well. Her father had taught her, she said. Her voice inhabited him. He wondered how she would sound between the sheets. He told himself to stop wondering because it was ridiculous and such things; instant, feral attraction did not happen to men like him.

When the eggs were safely transferred, the Prof asked him to take her to the rented house and she seemed happy enough to grab her rucksack and go with him. He envied her weightlessness, the way she travelled so light.

The house stood alone in the fields among the flat reed-bound lanes and ditches. There were groceries in the cupboard and butter and milk in the fridge. There was a bottle of wine too. She held it up to him and he nodded a 'Yes,' knowing he shouldn't drink at four thirty in the afternoon, or when driving.

'Just one,' he said. 'I'll keep you company.'

'Company?'

'So, you do not drink alone.'

'Ah, I see. I find some glasses.'

While she looked through the kitchen cabinets for wine glasses he got out his phone and sent a text, home. *Prob late 2nite, eggs delayed. Love F x*

He followed her into a room with two large sofas and a window onto the garden. They took a sofa each. They drank the bottle and talked about the project, she talked about growing up near the Elbe in her grandmother's house. He told her about moving up from London.

When the bottle was empty she wished for another but he said he'd have to go. 'But if you like tomorrow, I could bring more wine and cook for you,' he said.

'I like,' she said with a shyness that disarmed him.

He cooked her pasta with crab and they drank two bottles of Picpoul. When they finished eating they sat together on one of the sofas. There was a silence then. They were waiting, he thought. Both waiting. The air electric about them. He leaned across to kiss her but she pulled away.

'Are you married?' she asked.

'Yes. I'm married.'

'And you have a child?'

'Yes, I have a child. A boy, a baby, eight months.'

She sighed and turned away. She shook her hair and stretched her long neck, then turned back to kiss him and began to undo his shirt. When she lay on him, his hands moved over her back, feeling the wings of her shoulder blades, her narrow waist. He sucked at her neck, her skin tasted salty, she smelled of honey and lavender. When she came, she pulled away, arching back and crying out. Louder than he'd expected, a cry that seemed to come from deep in her throat. And he liked it, for there was no one to hear.

While she went to the bathroom, he went to the kitchen made them mugs of tea. When she came back, she took the mug from him and sat opposite him at the kitchen table.

'What is your wife's name?' she asked.

'Arleen,' he said.'

'Arleen,' she repeated, 'she is English?'

'Half English, half American.'

'Oh.'

He sipped at his tea.

'And what does she do?'

'She stays at home looking after our son.'

'I see. We shouldn't do this again, I think.'

'No, you're right, we shouldn't,' he said.

He was there the next morning before the sun was up, leaving Arleen and Jacob sleeping. After that there was no pretence. He came for her every morning to take her into the lab, where they played at being silent parents. They fed the newly hatched chicks to a background of birdsong and calling cranes. It was all about imprinting. About chicks not imprinting on humans. Not if they were to survive as cranes should.

Every evening he took her home and they made love

before he left. Some evenings he cooked for her but never stayed, although she wanted him to. He couldn't. Arleen would have known then for sure. He avoided thinking about what might happen, though he understood he could never be entirely happy again.

She didn't ask him to leave Arleen, although she wanted him to. She talked instead about leaving herself, about going back home once the project was completed and the cranes were making their own way in the wild. Then she would go back to the Elbe and its swamps.

The cranes were put out in the covered enclosure, a meadow area rich in spiders and worms. The fence was electrified to keep foxes away. They put their suits on. The suits were white and hooded and they carried sticks with painted wooden crane heads. This way they could guide the cranes, show them where to find food, how to feed. Run with them too. The young cranes took to them and at the slightest hint of danger hurried to gather around them, as a child to its parent.

He filmed it with the department's video camera. The success of the project was almost assured, barring any sudden catastrophe, which if it were to come, would be at their first flight. Would they fly off and never return?

'Why is the video camera still in the car?' she asked on their way home. Summer had arrived. The house was surrounded by meadow and corn. The garden blossomed with white poppies and a flower she did not know with pale lilac and pink blooms. She wanted to ask him to film her in the garden so she would never forget how beautiful it was. Secretly she thought they might one day own this garden. They might buy this house. Perhaps they could live here forever under the stars.

'I'm taking the camera home. Arleen asked me.'

'For what, for what purpose?'

He hesitated, he did not want to lie to her, 'To film Jacob. He's started walking.'

'Oh. That's good.'

'Yes.'

'I wanted...' she stopped.'

'What?'

'I wanted to dig the garden tonight. It's a beautiful evening.'

When he left she found some gloves and some garden tools in the shed at the back of the house and began pulling and digging up weeds and brambles, forking the fresh earth, uncovering earthworms for the blackbirds that hopped around her. She was thinking how the garden would look it's best and then she would ask him to film it, when she pushed her fork into the soil, put her weight on it and met resistance and the sound of metal, something other than soil. She dug down around it, by the time she had freed it she was sweating with the effort. It was an old and battered tin. It had been buried deep.

She knelt on the path with the tin in front of her, brushed the earth from the top and prised open the lid. Inside was a box, painted red. She lifted the box out and opened the clasp to reveal an egg. Nestling on frayed and worn silk, it was the size of a crane's egg, highly decorated and painted gold.

When he came for her in the morning she showed him the egg.

'It is treasure, no?'

'Yes, it must be. We should take in to Antiquities and let them see it.'

'In a day or two. I want to look at it first. Did you make your filming?'

He nodded.

'Shall we go upstairs? Is there time?'

'Why not?' he said and he took her hand and led her up. He wanted her then more than before, he wanted her as if he may never have her again. She was different, she smelled different, of the river perhaps. Her skin was feather soft and her cry was louder and more full-throated than ever.

The cranes are ready to be released. They are radio tagged and ringed. She is in her crane suit and they are following her out of the meadow pen so that they can at last fly. He and the professor are watching as the first crane opens its wings and takes off downwind. They stand hearts in mouths as it wheels in the sky and disappears behind a stand of trees. They will it to return, and sure enough it reappears, comes swaying in and lands directly at her feet. She wants to cheer but doesn't. No human voices to be heard. She is crane. They are all crane.

They celebrate the first flight by making love at five o'clock with the sun coming in at the windows, warming the stone of the old house.

At six o'clock he looks at his watch and says, 'I've got to go. I'm sorry but I promised.'

'Can you give me lift into town?'

'Sure. You going out?'

'For a drink with girls in the lab.'

'OK.'

He watches her dress. She looks taller. She puts on jeans and a grey silk blouse, and make-up. 'Ready,' she says.

He gets up and kisses the curve of her neck.

On their way through the kitchen she grabs sushi from the fridge.

The car smells of fish. He drops her in the town centre. He does not kiss her now for fear of being seen. Though he wants to. More than kiss. Hard to get enough of her.

'How will you get home?'

'Taxi,' she says and climbs out of the car. She waves and shakes her head and the silk of her blouse ruffles and floats in the air around her.

She is in the corner with the girls from the lab when he comes in. He doesn't see her. He is with a woman. He is with Arleen and another couple. They angle their way through to the bar. She can see them still. He puts his hand on the woman's back and rubs it gently. She watches as the woman turns to him and they kiss.

She gets up spilling her drink on her shirt. She has to go, she's sorry. She pushes her way out and onto the street. A cry is forming deep in her throat, like the cry of the crane in the swamp when it finds its eggs are gone. She hails a taxi to take her home.

Once inside she raids the fridge for the remainder of the sushi, rummages for frozen prawns, gnaws at some left-over chicken, crunching the bones, then downs a long glass of water. She packs her rucksack. She takes the egg from its box and clutches it to her as she curls up on the sofa. Tomorrow, before she leaves, she will take it to Antiquities. Though she may cry like a crane whose eggs have been stolen for a second time, she will do it. After all it does not belong to her.

In the morning she wakes to birdsong. When she gets up, she is unsteady on her feet. Her legs have grown long and spindly and her arms disappeared. In their place nubs of feathery wings are unfurling in readiness for flight.

There are students living there he thinks, judging by the music he hears when he drives past. He had tried to persuade Arleen that they should rent it, eventually buy it perhaps. She asked him if he'd lost his senses. So he let it lie. He comes often, alone. Sometimes simply driving past, sometimes pulling in and getting out of the car. She has been gone five months.

It is winter now and he stands by the ditch. The water is brackish and the reeds silvered with rime. His feet slip in the frosted grass. The sky above him has emptied of birds. Venus hangs low and bright in the sky. The evening star. He bends to pick up a long grey feather that lies in the grass, puts it in his pocket, then makes his way back to the car.

White Feather Girl

That he never once looked at me, that was part of it, though not all. And that he lived in the old stargazer's house, *the big house* some called it, a cut above us villagers. No match for a miller's daughter. It was that, and the times. They were different. The times had changed. Boots that had dug their way through the watery Fens, now ploughed the mud of Flanders.

I longed for a sign, each night as I undressed by the window and let the moon wash over me, I prayed for it. I looked out into the blackness known only to marshland. For the owl, hunting and quartering. For a whiteness of swans gliding in, their pale, bloodless forms skimming the fields, pearling the night air. I listened for the small things, the scuttling creatures, the voles and shrews, as they cried out, and I prayed that soon he would see me. And when I could pray no longer, I lay on my bed and let the wind in the sails and the low throb of the mill pump lull me to sleep.

When dawn came calling through the thin curtains, my prayers were forgotten. At five thirty every morning my mother shouted for me, 'Evie, it's time you were up,' and so I was, up out of my bed straight away.

'I'm coming,' I would yell, pulling on my boots. For I knew she would brook no delay.

That I had a bed to myself was a rare thing but I was the sole girl among four brothers, William, the only one not at war, had a club foot but it didn't trouble him much. He would run the mill once my father was no longer able.

Robert, the eldest, and Archie, the youngest, were in Belgium somewhere. Thomas was home with an infected wound in his leg that refused to heal. Mother washed it twice daily in carbolic and covered it in gauze smeared with paraffin wax. She let him sleep, when he could.

My first duty of the day was to fetch water from the pump, and milk which we got from a smallholding a half a mile along Upton Lode. After breakfast, I was to put the flat irons to heat in readiness for ironing Thomas's uniform. I did this twice a day in the hope of killing the lice. When it was ironed, my mother hung the uniform from a window to let the air get in. She would have hung it from the mill sails if she could.

After the ironing, I would work with my father in the mill or out in the fields. School was over for me, as it was for most girls coming up sixteen. When the day's work was done, and more and more of it falling to us young women, we knitted. We knitted socks, and as our needles clicked we dreamed of tall handsome fellas in khaki. Someone to knit for, sweethearts not simply brothers. We dreamed of the boys who had gone, of their adventures and we envied them their escape. They were travelling abroad. The village was deathly quiet without them. Girls danced with girls. There was no teasing or pulling of hair, no whistling, no horse play. Jumping in the lock and swimming was not the same that summer.

But the one I dreamed of, Michael Ramsay, was still at home. He had not signed up with the others.

Mary Cox whose father and two brothers were already gone, said it was a disgrace. 'Wasn't he as fit as the rest of them?' she demanded.

I told her he was and it was just a matter of time. It was just a matter of time before he noticed me, before he looked at me, before he made me his sweetheart and went off to war, like Robert and Archie with their brown paper parcels tucked under their arms, with their towels and shaving kits, waving goodbye when they reached the causeway, telling me to be a good girl and to look after mother.

I fell in love with Michael Ramsay at the fete for the Coronation. It was four years ago when I was just a child, barely past the May dolling and still at school and the Ramsays had come to live in the old stargazer's house. Michael was the only child, or so it seemed, and that was a rare thing in a world of families such as ours and overcrowded cottages, though we had the mill and that was more room than most.

Mr Ramsey was a history man from Cambridge. Michael would most likely follow in his father's footsteps, they said. He was destined to be a scientist, a stargazer perhaps, an astronomer of great fame. His mother, Mrs Ramsey, was rarely seen and said to be suffering from a rare wasting disease. Michael went to school in Ely, not with us. But every summer he came back, and every summer I waited for his coming and hoped that this would be the summer he would finally see me.

Michael Ramsay was broad in the shoulders, not like a man of learning, with hair the colour of ripe corn and green eyes. But I didn't know how green, how like a willow leaf in spring, until the morning he came for flour and my father called me to fetch him some eggs, for we always had a surplus. I took the eggs straight from the hen house. I kept them in the straw to save breakage as my cupped hands were shaking. I laid them, warm and brown, in his basket with the milled flour. He looked at my father and nodded and smiled. He half glanced at me and that's when I saw the green of his eyes. He thanked my father, then turned away. We watched him go.

'He's a fine lad, a shy one though, which is no bad thing in this day and age,' said my father.

That evening while Thomas slept after a draught of laudanum, my mother and I sat knitting in the kitchen. My father sat with us, head in his newspaper, and it seemed as good a time as any for my question. And so I asked, 'Why is it Michael Ramsay is still at home and not away with the rest? He has no brass badge. He's not essential like you.'

'I wouldn't know, said my father,' not lifting his head from his newspaper, 'that's between him and the recruiting sergeant.'

'The longer he stays the better,' said my mother looking up and holding her needles still.

'Why?' I asked.

'Why do you think?' she said. 'Because his mother needs him and she didn't bring him into the world to be sacrificed to the bullet in some foreign field.'

'Hush, they'll hear you,' said my father.

'As if I care,' she said. 'Damn them. Damn them all, the Kaiser and Kitchener. May they rot in hell. Damn the war,' said my mother and she spat in the fire. 'I'm going to bed,' she said and she put her knitting down without tidying the ball or the needles. Even though Thomas was back and William still at home, there was no pleasing my mother since her boys had gone.

That night, I lay naked in my bed listening to the wind whispering in the reeds. I thought how close I'd been to Michael Ramsey, close enough to touch. How he'd smelled of the morning and the heat that was to come. How the hair on his arms was golden and how his hands were twice the size of mine. I put my hands on my breasts and imagined they were his.

By harvest, Thomas's leg had healed, and on the day he set off to re-join his regiment we learned that Michael Ramsay's father, the history man, had left for France. Mary brought the news. My mother sighed, shook her head and said I was to go to the house with a basket which she filled with homemade elderberry jam, eggs, poppy tea and a freshly baked loaf. 'Women must stick together,' she said. 'The woman is an invalid, for God's sake, how is she supposed to manage?'

'And what of the harvest, we need every man?' said my father.

'It will be us, the women and children who get the harvest in,' she said.

It was then I decided. If women were to do men's work then why not? I would be bold. If he was there at the house, I would look into his green eyes and I would make him look at me. I would ask him outright.

When I got there, I saw him in the barn rubbing down the horse, his back to the open barn door. I stood in the entrance, breathed in the warm smell of hay and dung. 'Hello,' I said.

He stopped what he was doing and half turned. 'Oh, hello.' His hair was wet on his forehead and his arms glistened with sweat.

'We heard your father had gone. My mother sent me with a basket of things, for your mother, eggs and such like.'

He turned back to the horse and carried on rubbing it down. 'That's very kind of her. Thank you, please leave it there. I'll take it when I'm finished.'

'I was wondering,' I said, because I'd made up my mind if I wasn't going to fight for my country at least I could fight for what was in my heart, 'if you like swimming? Only, we're going for a swim tonight in the lock, me and Mary Cox, to wash the wheat off and we wondered if you'd like to come? It won't be until late after we finish in the fields.'

He turned back, nodded a yes and my heart began to thud like the mill pump. 'Thanks,' he said.

'Well, I'll see you there then. At seven, say.'

He nodded again but his back was to me now and his shoulder was bent into the horse's flank.

I told Mary straight off while we were sheaving and tying. 'We're for swimming in the lock tonight. I've got a date with Michael Ramsay.'

'No. Never. Did he ask you?'

'I asked him as it happens. I said we should meet up before he was off to the front. Told him you and I would be there at seven o'clock.'

'He's joined up then?'

'So I believe,' I said. And I believed it. Surely it was only a matter of time? No sweetheart of mine would be shirking the fight.

The sun stayed long over the summer fields, filling the sky, until it began to fall to the ground like the petals of a fading, red poppy. The water in the lock was still and clear as glass. Dragonflies clustered on the reeds at the edge where a grey heron stalked in anticipation. To my mind the world was never more beautiful or full of promise than the evening I was to meet Michael Ramsay.

We had our swimsuits on, Mary and I, under our clothes, and our towels under our arms. Would we wait, or would we jump in before he got there and watch him on the bank above us as he stripped down to his shorts?

We choose to go straight in the water and there was a fair amount of splashing and screaming. The heron flew off. Then we swam about for a bit and the sun-bloodied surface of the water settled into slow, gentle ripples.

I listened for him, for his boots in the dry grass. I watched for him, in a sky dazzled by the low-lying sun. I willed him, with all my might to come. I sent up a silent call, a prayer that I would see his silhouette appear on the bank above me. But the sun went down, the sky darkened, the water grew cold, and there was nothing for it but to admit that Michael Ramsay wasn't coming.

I told Mary there would be an explanation. His mother was an invalid after all. I made Mary swear on her grandmother's grave that she would not tell another soul that I'd been stood up, though I knew it was pointless. I knew tomorrow they would all know, villagers and harvesters alike. Our world was small.

I could not imagine a worse thing, or a greater disappointment. Imagination failed me. In the morning, my eyes were swollen and my heart was as hard as the root of the purple loosestrife. I cried off work that day and for once mother did not argue.

I knew where to go. Everyone knew it was the place for feathers, and white at that. It was under the plum tree at the edge of the village that feathers were found. Some folk said they belonged to a ghost bird, others that it was where the old gozzard had lived and plucked her geese. But I knew that this was a favourite spot of the swans from the Lode and their fledgling young. I was not disappointed, there were plenty of feathers to choose from and I choose the whitest, cleanest, softest swan's feather I could find and slipped into my pocket.

I told no one. I waited until Sunday, until chapel was over and the thin congregation spilled from the chapel doors. He came with his mother at his side. She was frail and bent and forced to lean on his arm.

I wanted to be sure that everyone would see, so I called his name out loud, 'Michael. Michael Ramsay.'

He looked across at me. His eyes met mine. For the first time, as I walked up to him he looked me straight in the eye. I took the white feather from my pocket and pinned it to his lapel for all to see. He blushed red and turned on his heels, pulling the feather from his jacket and throwing it to the ground. No matter. It was done. That Sunday, in that first summer of the war, I told the world that Michael Ramsey was a coward.

A week later I saw his name on the list in the church hall of those who had signed up. My mother said, 'I suppose you're satisfied now, are you? Sending a young man off to fight for his life, and what for?'

'The war will be over by Christmas,' I said and I saw us, Michael Ramsay and me on Christmas Eve, coming out from midnight mass, my hand in his, and I smiled and preened at the very thought of it.

Mary's father was the first, at Arras, then her brothers, both, at Neuve Chapelle. Archie at Ypres, Robert wounded at Loos, and though home, he barely speaks. He shakes with fright and refuses his crutches. Thomas is reported missing.

It is the same throughout our village and in every village and every county across the land. Our men are butchered in the Flanders mud.

These mornings the frosts are such that the reeds rattle and the birds freeze and die. We dare not think of the men and their hardships. We do what we can to keep the fire stoked and winter at bay. We feed and water the hens, fork turnips from the icy soil. There is nothing left to mill. We knit and darn until it is time for bed. Tomorrow is the fourteenth, Valentine's Day, a day for sweethearts. I sleep fitfully and dream of a meadow in summer. It is night and I am dancing under the stars as the feathers begin to fall. I watch them land at my feet. I stop and I crawl away.

When I wake in the morning it is to silent fields and hedgerows transformed by white. A thick, shroud of snow has fallen overnight, enough to cover a black corpse, enough to erase the blood that lies sticky beneath. After breakfast, I set off for the old stargazer's house, as I have most days since Michael left. The necessities I pull behind me on a sledge, milk, eggs and bread, whatever we can spare. I will take them to the back of the house and leave them by the kitchen door, as I always do. I will not knock. I will not go in. She will not have me inside. She will not look even look at me. And who can blame her? She is as bitter as the frosts and I am as lost as my brothers.

Flood

The winter of forty-seven is the harshest in living memory. Dyke, pond and land are frozen. The ground unyielding. Water-meadows teem with ice skaters racing headlong into the arctic winds. Pipes freeze and burst from their lagging and icicles hang from gutters and windows.

The Molly with their blackened faces and hobnail boots stay indoors. There is no dancing. None of the usual knocking and demanding of monies and beers. No furrows cut across the land. Even so, Francis is watching and waiting for them, for the men in women's clothing with their ribbons and rosettes. She is waiting to put on her boots and join in their pagan hullabaloo, to go out in the snow no matter how deep and celebrate.

Francis does not feel the cold, bitter though Bernard says it is. Its touch eludes her. Her other senses, smell and taste especially are heightened. For instance, she cannot bear the smell of Bernard's leather bag, even less its contents. Nor the medisoap he insists on using. She longs instead for the sweet scent of an orange, its colour, its juice on her tongue. But oranges are hard to come by. Instead she drinks rose hip, distilled from the hedgerows round about. In her pocket she keeps the handkerchief. It smells of summer and thyme.

The house is silent. Bernard has been called away to a difficult birth on the other side of the village. The father woke them that morning. When Francis opened the door at five am. she saw not The Molly but a desperate man, knee deep in a night's snow and in need of the doctor. She made him come inside and take a hot drink while she woke Bernard and he got dressed.

She did not go back to her bed. Now she waits at the window, rubbing away the frost so that she might look out onto a garden swollen with snow. In one hand she holds a teacup, the other rests on her belly. The sky is blanketed in cloud. The birds in hiding. Twigs and a berry or two protrude from the amorphous shroud. The world outside the window is dead and still. But here, inside her, life stirs. Out there may be ice and snow drift, frosted feather, and petrified bone, but here, inside, she is incubating a new life. Never mind that she is thirty-eight and already mother to a son, Robert, now ten years old. Never mind that the child in her womb is as unlikely as snow in May to be her husband's.

When she's had enough of waiting and is sure that no one will come, she lays down on the couch and sleeps. In the afternoon she makes a rabbit stew with winter celery and turnips for Bernard coming home. It's dark by the time she hears him come in and shake the snow from his boots and cap. He has delivered twins, one unlikely to survive he tells her in that matter-of-fact way he has of delivering bad news.

They sit to eat their stew.

Bernard says. 'Just think, in the summer it will be thirty years. It doesn't seem possible does it?'

He makes a point of never mentioning it by name, but she knows he is referring to Passchendaele and the shelling that had taken his leg, the leg of a young man barely seventeen, most probably saved his life because after that Bernard's war had been over. She'd asked him once if it was true about the rain and the mud and the horrors they'd heard of second-hand. He'd taken a sharp breath in and opened his mouth as to if to speak but then said nothing.

She couldn't blame him. What did she know? She'd been a child, no more than eight, taking posies with her mother to the shrine by the village hall where the names of the dead grew into an ever longer list. A child eavesdropping as adults whispered out of earshot, a child shrinking from her mother's grief at the loss of not just one but two brothers. The loss still to come of husband and father.

But this war, the one they'd just lived through, was different. In it, Francis had flourished. Catapulted from house and home, out of the yoke of domesticity and into the world of men, she'd relished her work with the Red Cross and the Wounded and Missing Service. Then all too soon the war was over, and women were supposed to go back to before, to make homes for heroes, as if none of it had happened, as if they had no say in their lives or futures.

She missed the Land Girls. Daisy and Alexandra had lived with them for the best part of three years. Now they were back in their own families and the youth, exuberance and laughter that had filled the house was gone. With Robert away at school and Bernard at work, there was only silence punctuated by the scurry of mice in the attic, the roosting pigeons and the grey dove that cooed in the rowan. And the clock's insistent tick that seemed but a heartbeat away from stopping. Bernard did not appear to notice the haemorrhaging away of her life blood, and Robert, when he was back from school, lived mostly outdoors with the boys from Holme Farm.

There were new recruits at the farm, Italian POWs there to help with the harvest, though it was hard to understand why anyone would stay in what some were calling a bankrupt land. When Robert came home with a toy plane carved from wood, and Francis asked where it had come from he said, 'From Claudio, at the farm.' He told her enthusiastically how Claudio and Giuseppe played football with the boys, how they were teaching the boys Italian, how the boys were teaching the Italians cricket.

She'd seen him first at harvest, a late summers day of cloudless skies and limitless space, the light translucent, the heat sufficient to silence the birds. He sat on top of the hay cart, pitchfork in hand. Robert was below on one side of the horse holding onto its reins. When Robert saw her approach, he waved and called out. Francis waved back.

Claudio waved too and called out, 'Ah Mama. Buon Giorno, Robert's mother.'

She nodded hello. She couldn't help but smile.

He jumped down and stood in front of her. There were drops of sweat at the neck of his open white shirt. His hair was curly and dark and slightly longer than it should have been. He made a small ceremonial bow, then looked directly at her. His gaze caught her out. She turned away and went over to the trestle table where the women were preparing a harvest lunch.

She kept her head down and set about cutting bread and cheese. Then Mary Johnson, who seemed to be in charge, gave her the tea pail and she took it around the men, holding it out for them to dip their tin cups in. When she came to Claudio, she determined not to look up at him so looked down at his boots, but his outstretched hand had brushed her arm and she raised her head instinctively. She saw it then in his eyes, the touch had been deliberate. No other hand had touched hers.

When lunch was eaten, the men lit up and everyone sat around smoking and chatting. Francis said goodbye to Robert and left.

She didn't join in the harvest that year. She told Bernard and Robert her back ached and needed rest. She stayed away from Holme Farm, but she saw him everywhere. It seemed impossible to go out and not see him, either on foot or on his bicycle, sometimes alone, sometimes with Guiseppe. Always smiling, always attentive. If they spoke, which they didn't always, he would ask after Robert. But once, when he was going into the surgery and she was coming out having taken Bernard his lunch, he told her how well the blue of her dress suited her, asking was it new, had she made it, did she know it matched the colour of her eyes?

It was at the Hokey, when the harvest was in, that she danced with him. First with Giuseppe but then with Claudio. It was hot in the marquee. He pulled a handkerchief from his pocket and offered it to her. She took it from him and wiped her brow. It smelled of the summer, of harvest and of thyme. He indicated she should keep it, then pulled her closer until she felt his breath on her neck.

Robert went back to school for the autumn term. Bernard was away in Cambridge at a symposium when Claudio came to the house to clear out the gutters. The ladders were left out in preparation. But they were not climbed. She took him upstairs, to the guest room, and watched him take off his shirt. He undressed her, and his kisses and the touch of his fingers imprinted themselves on her skin, so that even when he was gone, long after, she felt him there with her.

When Bernard asked why the guttering was still full of leaves she said Claudio had had to postpone the work but he would be coming again. Soon.

They met all through the autumn, snatching time in forgotten places: before dawn at the old barn beyond the farm, at the lock keeper's cottage, now abandoned, where they lit a fire and lay on the carpet under a heap of old quilts.

While the world around her prepared for winter, Francis blossomed like the plum in spring. She gave up all good causes and housewifely duties and took to the wild like a swan returning. A swan who had beaten her wings for thousands of miles and finally come home. She took no notice of the weather, battled the hag wind with the leaves tumbling around her, found her way through mist and fog to the Ponds where she swam naked, not feeling the cold through the heat of her arousal.

As a child Francis had dreamed of joining the gypsies who camped on the verges every year and sat by their night fires. Now that spirit child called her back. Now the unthinkable had become a possibility. She could burn down this life, the house, everything in it. She could break out of her captivity, she could run with Claudio. He had unlocked the reckless soul in her. A new and different life called.

He was not going home, he told her. There was no sweetheart, no one to go back for, though he would like to visit. Some day he would take her with him, he said, and she would feel the sun on her body and there would be no ice or snow.

On Christmas Day, Claudio ate with them. Giuseppe too. If Bernard suspected anything he didn't show it. He was the polite host and Robert enjoyed the Italians' company.

It was the first week of January when Francis began to suspect she was pregnant. And although she should have been alarmed, desperate even, her world was lit and her heart sang. The house came alive to her. In its whispers she heard the ghosts of children playing, of blackbirds tapping at the windows, of geese in the garden. She shared the tears of its women, their accumulated sorrows, the power of their dreams. She tasted poppy seed in her tea, feathers on her tongue, and in the violet depths of a clear night she saw a woman dancing in the meadow under the stars. Soon it would be her, dancing with the plough boys.

But The Molly did not come. Neither did Claudio.

Through February and into March Francis was forced to stay indoors, left to wait at the windows and watch the accumulating snow. When it finally stopped falling, rain followed, accompanied by the spring tides and then the thaw.

While Francis and Bernard sleep, the waters rise around them. In the morning Bernard hurries out to the surgery and when he comes home, he tells her that the rivers and ditches are full to bursting and that they must prepare for flood. They must move what furniture they can upstairs. That night they are kept awake by the deluge on the roof.

At midnight Bernard insists on going out. 'The men will be out scragging to build up the bank,' he says. 'They'll need as much help as they can get.' He dresses as quickly as he can, fastening his leg in place with its harness, pulling on trousers, shirt, sweater, and downstairs in the hallway his overcoat and boots. He has a spade and a storm lantern in hand and is about to leave, when Francis comes down, fully clothed.

'I can dig as well as any man. It's all our homes that are threatened,' she says. She pulls on wellingtons and an old mackintosh that flaps about her ankles, grabs a spade and battles her way behind Bernard who holds the lantern aloft into the night. They go out across the East Field to the ditch at Mill Lode.

Men are strung out along the banks of the lode, heads down into the driving wind and rain, digging furiously. The water is whipped into waves the like of which are more often seen on the North Sea. It threatens to spill at any moment. Bernard joins the gang. Francis jostles for a place and looks for Claudio. Surely the POWs will be here? It seems a few have gone to the village to fetch a pump from the boatyard. Perhaps Claudio is among them. But she cannot see him, he isn't here, but Giuseppe is only yards away, and when he sees her, he looks up and gives a small salute. Then he bends back to the already sodden soil and digs a shovelful from below the bank and piles it on top. They work like this in the hope of raising the lode side. No pump arrives and soon there is nothing more to be done but to trust in God and the elements. They down tools and straggle home to their beds. Shortly after dawn, the wind gets up and the waters top the bank. The village and its fields, the fen and carr quickly succumb.

Within a matter of hours, the flood waters reach the house, colonising the ground floor and creeping halfway upstairs. Bernard and Francis move to the bedroom and wait to be rescued. Francis lies on the bed and feels the child move within her for the first time. Bernard keeps lookout from the window. The following day the wind dies away leaving a pale watery sun to preside over the flood and a land transformed. The winter wheat and potatoes are gone and the bloated corpses of cows and pigs float by.

Then a rowboat. It is Giuseppe who comes. Bernard spots him and calls out from the window. When Guiseppe reaches them, he steadies the boat against the wall of the house while Bernard and Francis lower themselves out of the bedroom window down into the boat. When they are both seated, Giuseppe pulls on the oars and begins to row them across an inland sea that was once land.

'Claudio makes the best choice, I think,' Guiseppe says. 'He is right to go back. The weather at home is dry, warm also. Not like here.' He laughs. 'And maybe worse to come.'

'I thought you were both planning on staying here, for good,' says Bernard.

'Claudio change his mind,' says Guiseppe. 'He is, homesick, I think you say.' Guiseppe looks at Francis.

'Really?' says Francis. She feels in her pocket for the

handkerchief and crumples it under her fingers. She smells the scent of summer and thyme. Her feet recall the dancing. There will be no Molly now. She takes her hands from her pockets, clasps the sides of the boat and steadies herself as Guiseppe rows them across the flood.

A Morning Tide

We keep the table of tides hidden under the pillow, not sure we trust ourselves to decipher it, wait for the moon instead. Full moon high tide, our grandmother said. Steal out of the house risking everything and nothing. So what? We say, setting off across the estate into moonlit dark. There is a light on in the Campbell's house. Is Aidan asleep? Is Bingo awake? In the playground, the lunar glint of brass, the slide beckons, we climb up, hold our arms close, sail down feet first in a wind of our making. Over silent tracks, no night trains, sows sleeping. In the cowslip fields cows lying down chewing the cud. We follow the moon, lighting the dew as she does in the long grass that stains our plimsoles, our resilience abundant even in the dark. Up on the estuary, bay mud, the moon washing her face in the neap flood of a black tide, bowing at our feet. We are happy now, stirring stars in mud pools. Rescuing the small, white ghost crabs of ourselves. Waiting for what the tide might wash in...

We were three small figures come on a Sunday to worship the sea, myself, my brother Jack and his best pal Aidan Campbell. Stitched on the flood of a morning tide that filled the estuary, we gathered like creatures at the dew pond. And with us, as we stood plim-footed in the salt grass, me with my skirt hitched, was our dog Bingo, a one-eyed boxer. We stood alone in the wide, flat landscape. There were rarely others there, sometimes an occasional dog walker crossed our path but most of the dogs that lived near us took themselves for a walk. They were feral, as were we. We would sometimes come across lovers, half hidden in the long grass that bounded the rhynes but mostly it was just us in the still silence where time stalled and the silvery light that fused water, sky and land fell on us like a benediction.

We gathered here often, in our transient kingdom, a world away from the one inhabited by the adults in our lives, a world away from our mother Florence-Margaret...

Florence-Margaret was a young, black-haired beauty who wore French perfume and looked like Elizabeth Taylor, so she said. It was true she turned heads, a glamour puss in a world for the most part devoid of glamour. She was known as Margaret, though my father called her Marg. She'd taken her second name because her first, Florence, was 'too old fashioned' whereas Margaret, with its nod to a royal princess who was also the black sheep of the family, very much suited my mother's vision of herself.

Later, she told us all she preferred Maggie, but I could never bring myself to think or speak of her in this new incarnation. I'd been at her beck and call too long by then.

At fifteen, Florence-Margaret had been apprenticed to a tailor whose shop sat on the sea-front where the estuary opened its throat and you could watch the rise and fall of the tide on the sands below. She was a fine seamstress and made all her own clothes – Chanel suits, an apricot mohair coat, Dior evening dresses, all cut from the notoriously difficult Vogue patterns. By way of earning a living, while my father went to the factory, she sewed for the middle classes, for shopkeepers' and bankers' wives who regularly visited our house on the newly built council estate, out on the Levels.

The house spilled over with fabric, the dining table pulled out to its full length, silk laid, a pattern tacked on before the cutting, then stitching on the old treadle machine that played out the soundtrack of our days. I grew up with a love of material, in all its colour and texture, but I couldn't sew. She was too good for me to follow and she wasn't a teacher, impatient of my faults. This was the best of it, as I remember, our days out together shopping for material, later for clothes. My first dance and the dress she made me in three hours.

The worst of it is what happened behind closed doors, occasionally in broad daylight, and began long before we got to the estate, in the years before memory.

I bit her, so she said. I bit her nipples when I fed, though as far as I knew I had no teeth when I was born. It was painful, hadn't I hurt her enough? She hadn't known what to expect, any of it. How a baby emerged blood and caul in a disinfected, curtained world, and her alone on a bed. She told me this as if I knew full well what I was up to, responsible from day one, something she later liked to accuse me of – spoiling her fun. My grandmother clutched me to her and called me hers. I was spoiled and overfed.

I am three. We are crossing the road in Oxford Street, from my grandmother's terraced cottage to our flat. Where the road bends I run out and the milkman in his float, poor man, has to make an emergency stop. It's a terrible shock for him. I could have gone under the wheels. I could have been killed.

And that's why she gave me the hiding of my life – her words. Because I might have died. And that's why my grandfather stood in our kitchen that night, so she said, and told her if she ever beat me like that again he would take me from her. I guess she felt the need for confession. She didn't say she regretted it. I was left with the impression she considered it a demonstration of love.

Florence Margaret had very particular views on love. From the beginning she imparted her views and shared her confidences with me when we were alone in the new house, in the tiny kitchen with its walk-in pantry, Formica table and coke stove. By the time I was eight I was beginning to realise something was up, the world according to Florence Margaret was not a happy place and no hope for it. I didn't always agree with her, but I didn't dare say so. I didn't agree that there was no such thing as love, only sex. I wasn't really sure what sex was, even though she'd told me in some detail. I didn't see how it was all my father's fault that she was so unhappy. Or that women who let themselves go were disgusting, with their fat, slack bellies. I didn't enjoy hearing her name them, women I knew.

But in our small-kitchen-life it was me and her against the world. Only the two of us mattered. I was on her side. I shared her pain. It was a romance of sorts. Though I didn't want to hear about her lover ever, especially how he lied. Because then I'd have to admit I had something in common with him. By the time I was ten, I'd learned how to lie with the best of them.

'Let's play husband and wives,' said my new friend Jennifer, whose older sister was in the other room entertaining her boyfriend.

Jesus save me, I thought, but I didn't want a fight. Jennifer's ideas about marriage were different from mine. She lived in a different kind of house out on the Highbridge Road, detached with its own grounds. Her parents were away. Where did parents go, I had to wonder? To my surprise Florence Margaret had agreed I could stay the night, but I'd lied. I hadn't told her about the parents. So, when Jennifer suggested we kiss hello and kiss goodbye, that we lie down together on her bed and she kiss my neck, I panicked. Though I liked the gentle feel of her lips on my skin, I told her I had to go home.

When I got back, Florence-Margaret was unpegging washing from the line. I stood on the garden path and came clean, admitting I'd lied and saying I was sorry for it, though I didn't mention the kissing. I could tell straight away that there'd be no forgiveness. It was the way she had of looking at you, eyes dark lit with anger.

She told me to go inside and wait. I stood in the back room by the stove and when she came in, she put the washing down and set about me with a wooden hairbrush. I learned then that the truth was dangerous. I learned to lie and lie as if my life depended on it. Afterwards, I don't remember. I don't remember if there was pain or bruising – had it really been that bad? I don't remember if I cried. Most likely I went upstairs to Jack's room and we took the soft toys out of the big cupboard and played with them on his bed.

I didn't understand your anger, Florence-Margaret. Just as later I didn't understand why you tried to take your own life or what your cry for help was about. I did understand it was up to me to make you better and that's why I was kept off school to look after you. My yellow button-through skirt, pushing my hands deep into its patch pockets, spreading the material out from under its gathers. Hula hooping and loving the way it swung out around me. I didn't even mind that I was too plump to wear gathers. That you bought it for me, surely meant you were sorry, sorry for keeping me off school to keep you company when you were ill. Not that you ever stopped being ill or were ever better. It was a lifetime's work.

I'm standing on the desk in school in Mrs Baldwin's class, while she tells everyone to look at my new skirt – a present for looking after my mother. The eight-year-old with a mother in breakdown. What really happened? Was it me who found you, who sat on the bed with you and a bottle of tablets, empty, half-empty or intact? And the doctor, how did he get there? And my father saying you didn't have to go to hospital, that it was just a cry for help. Good girl that I was, I would stay home with you instead. I would be there to make sure you didn't take your life.

I took it seriously. Responsibility was my middle name. On reflection I'm not sure it was worth a yellow skirt. Walking down the street with you in South Avenue, I'm proud of my skirt and proud of you in your French pleat, Chanel jacket, red lipstick and high heels. How did it look? A twenty-nine-year-old posh bit and her yellow-skirted hostage of a daughter?

Our friendship didn't last. It was always one of those on off affairs. Nellie Gale, three doors down, to my mother, across the gardens: 'You haven't got that girl locked up in her room again, Margaret, have you?'

I hear her from the bedroom where I've opened the window to look out over the back garden, over cabbages and strawberries, waiting for the sound of my father's motorbike being wheeled through the entry, wishing him home.

More than anything I wished the fighting would stop, the drinking, the angry nights, the begging and pleading on my father's part. I wished she'd stop sleeping in the spare bed in my room, so I wouldn't have to be witness to it and pretend to be asleep. It got so being indoors was dangerous. It got so the world outside, especially the world of the estuary, became my sanctuary. A sanctuary I shared with Jack, Aiden and Bingo.

Jack and Aidan had found Bingo wandering by the railway track. He'd latched on to them and trailed them home – that dog knew a good thing when he smelled it. The Campbells had taken him in. It didn't matter that they had nothing and relied on charity including food parcels dispensed by Florence-Margaret and my grandmother Edith on behalf of the women's branch of the local Labour Party. It didn't matter that Mr Campbell, like Aidan, had suffered polio and was confined to a bed from which he rarely emerged and over which a steel and leather contraption was suspended. Once, delivering a box of groceries with my mother to their bungalow, I glimpsed him through the bedroom door and saw him haul himself up by the harness to sitting, then fall back onto his pillows from the very effort. He was known to be bad tempered and miserable and who could blame him? Though why he took it out on Aidan more than the others was impossible to know.

The Campbells were the poorest family in our street, on an estate where no one had much to shout about. But according to Florence-Margaret they'd brought their poverty on themselves. They had no business with a family that size. Five children were far too many and him an invalid, a wonder it could even be managed. Did she climb on top? He should leave her alone. Poor thing. But then they were Catholics, so what could you expect, my mother said.

It was a religion she had no time for, a religion she later told me, when I turned twelve, that had robbed her of her lover who lived several streets away – I'd somehow worked it out for myself by then – and who had decided to keep the faith and stay with his wife.

When it came to Catholicism, I was conflicted. Florence-Margaret was not. Take for instance the Pope, the way he made women suffer, the banning of condoms, it was a disgrace. As for doctors refusing you your right to terminate, she was vehemently against. I couldn't disagree with that. I knew that babies went missing in our street. Hadn't one disappeared in this very house, swallowed in a gin bath, a not yet born, small, ill-formed, slippery thing? It had to be as hot as skin could stand, she said, as much gin as a woman could drink – my father had helped – and quinine and castor oil daily.

I agreed it didn't seem right. I'd been glad of it, glad when she told me she was no longer pregnant. I already had Jack to look after, I didn't want a baby too. But secretly I held a candle to Catholicism. As I did to love, and women with slack bellies. Without them, what could I hope for? I envied the lace gloves and Sunday veils of my Catholic cousins. I envied the Mass and the confession. And I longed for a school hidden behind high walls, with a name like La Retraite, exotic in our world. A world where so much was forbidden.

When he and Aidan found Bingo, Jack knew that Florence-Margaret would never take him in. It went without saying that there would be no dogs adopted in our house or cats or any dirty, unbiddable creature and certainly not a stray. There would be nothing to dent the image of relative prosperity, after all we had a car, at least when it started, and many on the estate did not. But I would not have wished it on a dog anyway, not in those times when being indoors was like walking barefoot on broken glass. What animal could do that day after day and not be harmed?

To be outdoors was to walk on solid ground in a world of our making, altered only by the tides. I always knew by the time we reached the hawthorn ditch if there was water. I could smell the sharp sting of the silent, salt lake lapping at the grass and I could smell its absence; mud as far as the eye could see, silvery mudbanks that smelled of iron and blood. The smell of hours lost, spent wandering its dangerous margins. The scent of Sunday when tensions in the house inevitably rose to boiling and we were sent outside to disappear. Even before any hint of dinner. Do not come back, the unspoken message.

Sunday was the one day in the week my father was at home. The one day my parents could not escape each other. Every other day he went to work on his motorbike, gone before we got up, arriving back when we were in bed, or at that time of day with nerves shot and unable to cope any longer, she would have banished us to our rooms. Sunday was the day the old green B.S.A. stayed propped against the back of the brick shed and my father sat in the front room with the newspaper and a cigarette while my mother cooked what seemed a hellish concoction of burnt beef, brown gravy, slimy roast potatoes and mashed cabbage. How later, in her evening cookery classes, she could make the exquisite custard tarts and choux pastry was a revelation to me.

Aidan hated Sundays as much as we did. And who could blame him. After all, which of us would want to go to Mass and hear about God's love and forgiveness when he'd been lumbered with a wooden leg? We all knew about the leg, though only Jack had seen it. Aidan didn't make a big deal of it. He was as much a daredevil as the next boy. I thought about it sometimes, how and where it was strapped on. I'd seen a brace, my cousin from the Welsh valleys wore one, but a whole leg, that was different. It must have been a relief to take it off at the end of the day. Did it rub and chaff like my legs sometimes did in the summer, which came of being fatter than I should have been, which came of spending stolen moments in the walk-in pantry dipping my fingers into the Nestlé Condensed milk tin and scooping it onto my tongue.

Aidan had lost his leg to polio. We all knew about polio; how deadly it was. How it could wither your limbs, how it could steal your breath and you could end up in an iron lung, a machine that looked like a diving bell that swallowed you whole. I imagined with horror how it would be to lie paralysed and alone, encased in this tomb, with only your head sticking out. What if you needed to scratch an itch? Was there room to move? Could you speak? Did you ever come out? How did you go to the toilet? Maybe you didn't because they didn't feed you. Maybe you wore a nappy, surely not?

Rumour had it that polio was carried by stray cats, another compelling reason for our unspoken no dog, cat, animal policy. It was also rumoured to come from overseas in crates of bananas. I don't remember if bananas were allowed in the house.

When my mother thought there was a chance I might have polio, she sent me to my grandmother, Edith, to be looked after. Edith sent for the doctor and they stood whispering at my bedroom door. I heard the word mentioned, I heard the doctor say an emphatic, 'No.' Then it was bliss, a whole fortnight of my grandmother's dedicated care, washed daily in lavender water, warm and fed ensconced in her big old-fashioned bed, I had nothing to concern myself with but my own comfort.

The tide was already retreating when we arrived on the riverbank that Sunday morning. Aidan and Jack took to running about and throwing small crabs at each other. Bingo disappeared into the hawthorn ditch where we imagined he chased rabbits, though if he did, we never saw him catch one. I wandered as far as the pill box and sat on the marram grass, looking out to sea, dreaming my sea dreams. I liked the silence broken only by the gulls. I liked not having to be on guard, no listening out.

But the silence was short-lived, broken by Jack shouting for me. I turned to see him running towards me, 'Aidan's got his leg stuck. Quick, quick,' he called. I saw Aidan then, half on the bank, half in the mud and Bingo stood over him. I ran back along the bank with Jack and got there as Aidan was wriggling out of his trousers and unstrapping his leg. The abandoned leg, all wood and leather, all bandage and strap, was sucked into the mud and slowly disappeared before our eyes. We knew about quicksand. We knew how it swallowed cars whole, so they said. It was dangerous. As far as we were concerned the leg was gone and there was no hope of getting it back. Jack and I pulled Aidan to safety, so the whole of his body lay on the bank. I tried not to look at his stump, its fleshy, withered, pinkness.

We were a sorry, muddy group, Aidan hopping and leaning on Jack, returning over the fields and through the estate. There was no way, Aidan said, that he could face telling his father he'd lost the leg. There was only one thing for it and that was to throw ourselves on Florence-Margaret's mercy and pray she'd take pity on us. It was a risk. I knew she wasn't fond of children and preferred them seen and not heard, but she had a soft spot for Aidan. I think she admired his spirit, a spirit which in her own children she would have found unthinkable and in need of dampening.

We stood at the back door, which was open due to the heat and the cooking. The smell of charred meat wafted around us. We told her the tale of the leg and I caught the rare glimpse of a smile cross her face. She said we'd better come in and she called my father. Leaving the meat and potatoes in his care, she sat Aidan down on a kitchen stool and cleaned him up. She sent us upstairs to get washed and changed. Once Aidan had dried off, Florence-Margaret took him home.

When she returned, we sat down to dinner which we ate in silence, hardly daring to breathe, knowing we'd got off lightly. After dinner she banished us upstairs to our rooms and there was nothing to do then but stay quiet and pray for the silence and peace to last.

Nothing to do but wait for the day's end, for darkness to fall, to creep out under the moon, to see what the mud might give up and the tide wash in...

Millie and Bird

It was the kind of summer when the grass grew too long to cut and your toes stubbed at the damp end of your trainers, the summer I was sixteen. It rained all through May and June. It rained on my birthday. It never let up and the weeds in the yard grew taller than the gate post. Jonty Angel, our next-door neighbour, gave Millie the bird that summer, a white zebra finch, and she spent all her time coaxing it onto her shoulder, whispering to it and feeding it titbits. He gave her a cage too and she put it in her bedroom out of harm's way. It was the summer of Bird, it was the summer I fell in love.

'Why the hell does she have to go round the house with that stupid bird on her shoulder, for Christ's sake? What girl her age does that?'

'I don't know but she's only thirteen. Where's the harm?' I say.

'When I was thirteen I had better things to think of, like school for one thing. No time for pets. No time to whisper sweet nothings at a stupid bloody bird.'

I watch Millie walk into the yard and up through the garden, Bird on her shoulder, its beak buried in her hair. She disappears behind the shed. Behind the shed it's mostly overgrown with nettles. There's an old crab apple, a sink which coats over every spring with a skin of spawn, a rusty bike and a couple of broken cold frames.

'Why don't I make you a cup of tea Mum? See if there's

anything on the radio, a concert or something? There might be a play on.' I say.

As if she doesn't hear me she goes to the sideboard, opens the door and reaches inside to the stash she keeps behind the pile of old records we're not allowed to touch. She lifts it out like she's won a raffle, like it's a surprise, like she didn't know there was a half-full bottle of vodka there. She pours herself a mug, holds it up and smiles like she doesn't ever need to be put to bed, or ever get sick, or rant and rave about it all being our fault.

I go out into the garden and look for Millie. I won't go behind the shed into the nettles as I don't want my legs all messed up with stings. I want them silky smooth and ready for the fake tan. 'Millie, what are you doing?'

'Nothing.'

'Come over here then and sit for a bit.' I'm on the bench in front of the shed. It moves when you sit on it. The grass is shorter here on account of it having to work its way up through crazy paving and gravel. 'Come on.' I want her to come but not for her sake. I'm not worried about her getting nettle rash and besides she's got Bird. That's what she calls the bird: Bird. When I asked her why, she said it seemed for the best, that naming leads to attachment and I said where the hell did she get that idea from, and she said she read it on the internet.

Mille sits next to me. Bird is on her shoulder moving from one red foot to the other like he's stepping up and down in time to music we can't hear, clawing at her t-shirt. He turns his head and looks at me with a black eye. I think about Otis and his smoky, black skin that smells of walnut and vanilla.

'You going out tonight?' asks Millie.

'Yes, seven o'clock, Elaine's first, we're meeting there then going into town.'

'Can I come?'

'Don't be daft you're thirteen.'

'Well *you're* only sixteen and one week.'

'Next year maybe, anyway I don't think Bird would appreciate it, in Jelly's, with all that noise and all those people.'

Bird is still now. A cabbage white floats past and a swarm of midges hover above the long grass. I think I should do something about the grass, like ask Jonty if I can borrow his mower, though he said it needed to be cut down first. A crow flies out of the lilac tree above us and Bird jumps up onto Millie's head.

'Is it stupid or what, that bird? It'll get eaten by the crows if it's not careful.'

'He's just nervous,' says Millie and puts her hand up and grasps the bird and brings it down into her lap where she cups it in both hands. 'His heart's beating like crazy,' she says, 'feel it.'

She goes to pass the bird to me but I pull away, 'don't give it to me,' I say, 'I don't like birds.' But it's not that I don't like birds, it's that I don't want to feel its heart beating like that, not when its skin is all feathers and a puff of wind coming by could break its bones.

'What's not to like? He's beautiful, feel him, he's like silk and he smells of grass.' She holds the bird towards me.

'Don't bring it near me,' I say. 'Keep it to yourself. Come on, I'll make us tea before I go out.'

I make egg and chips because it's easy, oven chips cook themselves. It's just for us. Mum's in the front room with the telly and her bottle. Millie feeds the bird a chip. He's not normally allowed at the table. We clear away and then go upstairs to my room. Millie puts Bird in his cage and then comes and sits on the bed and watches me get ready. We share a bottle of coke and I smoke a cigarette out of the window as best I can, but it's hard because it's raining and the cig is getting damp.

Millie does my nails with the purple varnish I bought especially. She's good at doing things like hair and nails although you wouldn't think so to look at her. 'You could be a hairdresser or a beautician,' I say, 'if you weren't so brainy.' She smiles. Millie is clever; the cleverest girl in her class, although how she's going to be anything beats me. I used to think about being a lawyer. I fancied that, but now, well I'm not sure. Jonty Angel says he might be able to get me a job in the auction house where he works. Sometimes you have to be realistic and scale things down, the kind of things you'd been hoping for. I used to pray about that kind of stuff but then your prayers they get rained on like the grass.

I like it when Millie takes my hand and then each of my fingers, one by one, and holds them while she paints the nail. She's just dipping into the thick, pearly varnish when we hear stumbling on the stairs and the bathroom door banging shut. Millie puts the brush back in the bottle and we wait. I listen hard. I'm good at listening, it comes with practice. I've got dolphin ears. Dolphins hear fourteen times better than humans. After a minute or two we start up again and one by one my nails take on a glossy purple sheen. I look at Millie, at her bitten-down nails and I think – tomorrow I'll paint them purple.

The toilet flushes and the bathroom door opens. Her bedroom door closes. 'She's gone to sleep it off,' I say. 'She'll be snoring like an old bag lady soon.' Millie stops, brush midway between bottle and the little finger of my left hand. I can tell she doesn't like what I've said. But I laugh and before long she laughs and then we both laugh and we roll about on the bed laughing, only not too loud and me with my hands in the air to stop my nails smudging.

'Can I wait up for you?' Millie says.

'It'll be late.'

'I'll get into your bed.'

'Not with that bird you won't.'

'I'll leave Bird in his cage. Promise.'

'All right then.'

It's gone eight when we wake in the grey light. I hear the rain outside and a cheeping noise at my ear. What the hell. I told her no bird.

'Millie,' I turn. The bird hops away from my ear and onto Millie's pillow. 'I thought I said no bird.'

Millie opens her eyes. 'I couldn't leave him. Mum got up after you went out and came downstairs and said I'd got to give Bird back to Jonty or else she'd get rid of him. I was scared she'd hurt him.'

'Well put him back in his cage now or get his box or something, just get it out of the bed.' I turn over and push my head back in the pillow and replay last night's kiss, and then I hear her.

'Breakfast!' She shouts up the stairs, 'Come on, up you get.'

I turn back to Millie and raise my eyebrows in a kind of here-we-go-again way. 'Better get up,' I say. 'It's going to be one of those *happy-family days*.'

No one makes pancakes like she does and she's cut up fruit and there's syrup and sugar and lemon and a clean cloth on the table.

When we finish eating, she says, 'The rain's stopped. Think it's about time we saw to the garden. There's a scythe somewhere in the shed. I'll find it. You go next door and borrow Jonty's mower.'

It's true, the rain has stopped and the sun is out and it's warm enough to be outside in a t-shirt, and I don't care that

I've had less than five hours' sleep, what with getting in so late, because I'm in love and, as it turns out, it is one of those *happy-family-days* and who knows when the next one might come around.

The garden looks different by the time we finish, like it's doubled its size. The sky is cloudless and we've got the old car rugs out on the lawn. Mum reads the paper. I doze on and off and think about Otis walking me home. I think about him kissing me in the lane; kissing Otis is like sucking chicken from a bone, and I think about how when I went round to his house his Mum made us a whole plate of chicken sandwiches for supper. If things carry on like today, *if*, then maybe I can invite him back, that's what I'm thinking when I hear the click of a lighter and look up to see Jonty leaning on the fence.

'All right girls? Looks a bit more like it,' he says, lighting his rollie with the Zippo flame. Jonty's got a pierced tongue and a tattoo of an eagle on the back of his neck and he's wearing a t-shirt that says *The World is Disappearing*. It's black and it's got a line of blue-green worlds across the front that get smaller and smaller until they disappear round the back. I used to think Jonty was a messenger. Well for one thing 'angel' means messenger, Millie told me that, and for another, because of his t-shirts which said things like: *I Just Wanna Be Myself, Love Kills, No More Pain*. I used to think he was speaking to me until I realised he was the drummer in an old punk-rock band and it was his uniform. He doesn't play in the band anymore on account of him nearly losing his foot in a motorbike accident.

I wonder if Jonty is really worried about the world disappearing: the land sinking, the seas rising, polar ice caps melting. I know all about it from school and Mrs Allen in geography but I can't be worrying about it. I've got too many other things and besides it's not exactly news to me;

my world's been disappearing from as far back as I can remember, mostly into the bottom of a vodka bottle. Today, just for once, I wish Jonty was wearing something to make us smile, like that t-shirt of his that says, *If You Want Breakfast in Bed, Sleep in the Kitchen,* or best of all, the red one with, *Save the Drama for Your Llama*, in big white letters across the front.

'Fancy a barbie? I've got a few burgers in the freezer, veggie as well as meat.'

Millie's eyes light up. She likes being around Jonty, we both like being around Jonty because you can rely on him. Jonty is reliable which you have to be if you've got an aviary full of birds to look after. Millie is the only one he lets help him. Mum likes him too, she's known him since she and Dad first moved in, further back than we can remember. Sometimes they play old records together, sometimes he calls her *Blondie* and you can tell she likes that.

'Come on then before it decides to set away raining again. I'll get it lit. If you want ketchup you'll have to bring it with you.'

By the time we've eaten our burgers the sky is the colour of wet tarmac. We sit sipping coke and waiting for the rain. Nobody speaks. I'm praying it won't rain, praying for the end of the summer when rain washed the baby wood pigeons out of their nests in the plane trees and into the gutter. I think of Otis and I pray: let every day be like today, so I can bring him home; no more sideboards and vodka, no more coming in from school and her sparked out on the sofa. I let that fantasy loose in the air around me and I wonder if we're all, in our own way, dreaming of the same kind of thing. I'm sure Millie is because she's got that faraway look and a half-smile on her face and for once she isn't petting Bird.

'We should go away on holiday,' says Mum, 'get away

from this sodding, sandbag summer, somewhere hot ... Greece. I went there once with your Dad.'

I hold my breath.

'Let's drink to it,' she says.

We all hold our breath. Jonty gives me a quick look then says, 'Aye, good idea, why don't I make us a cup of tea?'

Jonty brings a pot of tea and a packet of digestives on a tray with four mugs. We drink tea and listen to the birds shushing and chirruping in the aviary. The rain clouds pass and the sky turns blue again and I'm starting to think that everything seems OK and maybe I'll get out tonight, so I take my phone out of my pocket. I'll text Otis, who knows I might even go round his house for a bit. And I'm thinking how his Mum might make us chicken sandwiches again for supper, when I look up and see Millie's gone.

Don't ask me where it comes from or why but I can feel it, like a wild animal feels the coming storm, something moving on the air; it's my dolphin ears and most likely my nose too. I know something isn't right. I put my phone down. 'Where's Millie?'

'Gone to put Bird away,' says Jonty, 'she's going to give us a hand feeding that lot,' he nods in the direction of the aviary. Mum's drinking tea and smoking, her head buried in Jonty's newspaper. She doesn't look up as I get to my feet.

I call for Millie in the house but there's no reply. I walk through the garden, following my dolphin nose, down to the shed, then round the back to the nettle patch. Mille is there, squatting by the old sink with her hands in the water.

'Millie, what's up?' I say but I don't need an answer because Millie takes her hands out of the water and I can see what's up, right there, under that clear blue sky, shining in the sink, I can see it, see him: Bird, floating lifeless, his feathers slicked onto his tiny body. 'Millie, what, how...?'

111

'I'm going to take him out now, find something to wrap him in, then bury him.'

'But Millie, what happened?'

'Some things are too hard to bear,' says Millie laying his body on the grass. 'Some things you just couldn't bear.' She looks up at me with a look that says – *you know what I mean*, and I don't need to think about it because I do. I know exactly what she means.

I nod. 'We'll bury him,' I say. 'Then you can go and help Jonty with the aviary, and after that I'll paint your nails purple.'

Millie already has a trowel and she's digging a hole at the base of the crab apple. She takes an old crepe bandage from her pocket and wraps it around Bird. She lays him in the hole and covers him with wet leaves and soil. 'Say a prayer,' she says. And I do.

Dancing with Mr Benn

I don't remember it raining that summer although it must have. There must have been thunder. I remember lilac against a pewter sky and its thick scent filling the garden. Perhaps it rained. Other summers when it rained, we holed up in the shed and sat on the old canvas chairs with the door open watching the rain fall. Efa didn't like to retreat to the house and only did so when it was time to make Jack's tea for him coming in from work.

Efa wanted to be a nurse. Her father said, 'No good woman was ever a nurse.' So that was the end of it. She told me while we stood in the shade looking down at the pale wings of the yellow poppies, Efa whispering a benediction over them in Welsh. It was the summer of 1959, a year when the sun came early and stayed late, and we were together in the garden every day. I was ten and I'd caught a fever and been brought to her house. 'Polio,' they whispered at my bedroom door but after a week of my grandmother Efa's care I'd recovered.

My temperature was normal but Efa still washed me in lavender water to keep away the heat and sang to me in that strange lilting language of hers. A language she used only in the garden. Jack, my grandfather, forbade the speaking of Welsh in the house and if a word slipped out, as it did sometimes, when she forgot herself, he raised his fist to her and Efa's face went white as the snow-in-summer that grew in the rocks by the shed. But he didn't hit her, not if I was there. Efa said Jack didn't like the Welsh.

All summer we carried water in buckets and in the watering can, filling them up from the cold tap at the kitchen sink, lifting them up and out, over the flood-step into the yard. From there, once past the coal bunker and the mangle we were onto the brick path that ran the length of Efa's garden. In my child's eye it was a long way to travel to reach the chicken coop and the shed at the end. It was only later that I came to see the narrowness of the garden, the long, cramped beds, the lack of grass.

I carried my own small bucket which was blue and also the bucket I took to the beach. Efa who was stout and aproned with coarse, wavy hair and apple cheeks, carried two full buckets at a time, arms and hands taut under the weight, me following behind watching the water spill from the bucket brim and form dark spots on the brick.

'There's always something needs doing in a garden,' Efa said.

That year it was watering. We watered before the sun got going, as long as Jack was at work, and again in the early evening when he took the dog down to the sands. We filled the two old sinks used for dipping and the saucers we'd troweled out round the beans and peas to hold water. Likewise the roses especially the Ena Harkness that smelled of fruit and that Efa was training up over the old timber of the chicken coop. The dark peonies too, although Efa said 'No drowning the peonies, they're fussy, don't like too much water.' And then the sweet peas and strawberries. We watered everything but the yellow poppies. Poppies are survivors, Efa said.

'Why doesn't Jack like the Welsh?' I ask Efa as we sink down into the green striped deck chairs by the rhubarb. Efa is picking over the loganberries she's collected in a colander, looking for grubs.

'He's different see,' she says. 'Not one for reading or singing is Jack. Didn't like the yard covered in coal dust nor how he had to spend the night killing blackclocks and cockroaches with his best shoe.' She starts to laugh then. 'What a sight he was and his first visit to the Valleys, the night of our honeymoon it was.'

I know well enough why Jack doesn't like the Welsh. It's one of the stories Efa likes to tell. There were the insects and the coal, he knew nothing about miners, and he thought he was better than them, which he wasn't because, well just because, Efa always stopped short there. He was jealous of her brothers she said, especially Bryn who died in the war. Sometimes Efa brought her red leather writing case out into the garden and showed me the picture she kept of Bryn. There was another tucked in behind it, not much larger than a postage stamp, a different man but in a uniform like Bryn's. This man had black, shiny hair and a smile. He was a friend, of her brother's, she said.

'Here,' says Efa and she scoops loganberries from the colander and offers them into my cupped hands.

Now when I'm in my garden it's my hands at work that make me think of Efa. Hers always busy, a brace of fat breasted pigeon, the colour of the pink japonica on the sunny wall where the fruit canes were planted and the honeysuckle grew. Efa's wrinkles and liver spots and her blue veins are mine.

Efa rubs her hands across her brow and then her apron. 'Phew, it's a hot one again, I'll take these inside,' she says lifting the colander. 'I'm going to fetch my writing case. I've an important letter to write. See if there are any eggs why don't you?'

I get up, go over to the coop, reach inside to the warm straw and feel for eggs.

'No, eggs,' I say as Efa comes back with her writing case in one hand, her other outstretched to graze the herbs that are growing alongside the path. Then under her breath – mintys, persli, rhosmari, teim – she whispers their names. When she reaches the rhubarb she puts her writing case on the deckchair and walks to the garden's end where the yellow poppies grow and talks to them in words I don't know. We sit back in our deckchairs. Efa has a cushion on her lap and her writing pad.

'Who are you writing to?' I ask. 'Is it about them wanting you to be on the council like you said?'

'No, it's a letter to a very important person, to Mr Tony Benn, Mr Anthony Wedgwood Benn to be exact. He's in Parliament and I'm asking him to come here to the Labour Party dance. They think I'm mad but we'll see. They won't think I'm such a fool when I'm away dancing with him.'

'Does Jack think you're mad?'

'Ssh child, Jack doesn't know.'

We whisper then even though Jack is away out at work, probably somewhere miles off laying bricks for the council.

'What if he reads it?'

'Jack doesn't,' she says, 'he's not one for reading.'

'Can I look in your writing case?' I say. It's on the path next to Efa's chair. She's zipped it back up.

She picks it up and hands it to me. 'Careful,' she says.

It's hot from the sun. I unzip it slowly to catch the breath of its secrets, the little things hidden in its pockets, like stamps and photos the size of stamps, the Vote Labour biro pens, the blue vellum envelopes. I look first for the folded letter and the medal from the Red Cross. Efa was in the Red Cross in the war. She stayed at home like Jack but she learned to be a nurse.

'Is this what they gave you when they called your name out in the hall, when you were stood at the back and you couldn't believe it? When they said you were the best nurse out of all the cadets?'

'It is,' says Efa looking up from her writing pad. She smiles. 'It'll be yours one day.'

'I might not be a nurse,' I say.

'You can be anything,' says Efa, 'you could go to the university.'

I look at the photos. There's one of the big house where Efa worked when she came from Wales. Where it was all polishing and dusting and cooking.

'Tell me about the house Efa, tell me about Vera,' I say holding up the photograph.

'Oh Vera, just because she lived in a big house in the Quantocks always had to have clotted cream for tea and caviar for breakfast. Proper lady, never washed her hair though, right down her back it was. Her fiancé died in the war and she cut it off with the garden shears. What a garden that was, puts this to shame, and the grass, acres of it like the valley. I miss that, the smell of summer grass, the wide open spaces.'

'There's grass on Jack's allotment,' I say, 'by the pigeon cree.'

'You call that grass?'

Efa told me it was Jack who'd saved her from service and the big house. He came along, young and handsome so she married him. There's a photo of Jack holding one of his prize pigeons, in the writing case, as well as one of my mother and me when I was just a baby in the pram, and my uncles in their uniforms including my uncle Terrence, her youngest son, with his motorbike before he moved to Canada.

'Did you miss him when he left?' I hold up the photo of Terrence.

'Like a stone in my heart it was. I told Doctor Watkins – too many stones, I said when I went to the surgery and he gave me something. It helped for a while and then well, there was nothing to be done, so I got on with the planting and the poppies, yellow of course,' she said and then something in her language. I remember gyfer and golli, something about loss, and there were three names, Bryn, Terrence and I never could catch the other but I had an idea who he was.

It must have been the heat that made us lose track of the time and suddenly the latch on the back gate lifted and Jack appeared wheeling his bike in through the yard. Efa jumped up, put the writing pad back in the case zipped it up and said to me, 'Stay here.'

But Jack was already on the brick path and the garden was shrinking around us.

'What time do you call this? Nothing better to do. Time for the young uns tea and you're out here with that bloody writing case, as usual. Who've you've been writing to? Better not be Lionel Davies, you'd better not be writing to the council Efa. I've told you no wife of mine'll ever be on the bloody council. Labour Party's bad enough.'

'I'll make your tea,' she said. 'Why don't you go across to the allotment and feed the pigeons.'

'I'm going nowhere until I've had something to eat,' he said standing in front of her.

Then he bent down picked up Efa's writing case and turned back along the path. When he came to one of the old dipping sinks that was still full of water he threw the writing case in and pushed it down below the green scum and the watermark to make sure it was submerged.

Efa let out a small cry.

He turned, 'Leave it,' he said.

'Stay here,' she whispered and she followed him in.

I watched them disappear into the yard, waited until I knew they would be through the back door into the kitchen and then made for the sink and fished out the case. I took it to the end of the garden and sat behind the chicken coop on the rocks by the snow-in-summer. It was cool and hidden in the shade. I listened hard there was no shouting from the house only the chuck-chuck of the chickens and over by the raspberry canes, in the sun, a blackbird singing.

I dried the case on my shorts and unzipped it. Water had seeped inside and the blue vellum paper was blotched and the ink had run. The letter was ruined. I put it down, went round to the coop and let myself in. I picked up the old tin tray that Efa sometimes used for grain and bread. I shook it clean and let myself back out with the tray under my arm. I picked up the case and the tray and moved into the sun along the rows of strawberries to where there the old cloche sat with its broken panes. I knelt down in the warm soil, took everything out of the writing case: the photos, the folded letters, the stamps… I spread them on the tray, put tiny stones that I raked from the soil on each one and then carefully lifted the tray into the cloche to dry. I put the writing case in too, then went in for my tea.

I sat by Jack and ate from his plate of cockles. His mood had improved and grew better still when Efa produced a warm blackcurrant tart puddled in cream. Efa ate nothing but when Jack got up from the table and said he was away over the allotment she listened for the front door slamming then made herself a cup of tea and some toast and poured me lemonade. The house breathed.

'Don't worry,' I said to Efa, 'I've got your writing case.'

We went back out into the garden. I crumbled the head of a lavender stalk through my fingers as we walked up the path. The shadows had lengthened, they flickered in the breeze that had sprung up. The tide would be on its way in said Efa. But it was warm still on the sunny side by the wall and there were cabbage whites and red admirals and the smell of night-scented stock that Efa had sewn by the rhubarb patch. I showed her the cloche.

'Good girl,' she said. And put her arm round my shoulder and squeezed me. 'We'll leave it there for now. Take it in with us later.'

'The letter's spoiled,' I said.

'Never mind,' said Efa.

I open Efa's writing case. Even now it smells of her. It smells of lavender and rhubarb. Beneath the half-empty packet of poppy seeds and the picture of her brother's friend is the letter from Mr Benn, who would, he says, be delighted to attend the annual Labour Party dance. And the photograph. Efa is wearing the dress my mother made her. It's a black dress. She's wearing it with a silver poppy brooch and a pearl necklace and she's dancing with Anthony Wedgwood Benn.

How the Sea Can Save You

When she gets angry like this I turn away. I don't want to look at her. I don't like looking at her at the best of times, even though they say she's a beauty with film star looks – at least that's what she says they say. It's those black eyes of hers and their do-not-defy-me spell that scare me, and the angrier she gets, the darker her eyes grow; green to black, leaf to crow.

I wish it was different. You're meant to love your mother. I know. You're meant to want her near you, but she has a habit of getting too close, so close I can smell her breath. She pushes and prods at me as if my body is not my own, as if like everything else it belongs to her and she's entitled to pinch and bruise. And saying anything only makes it worse.

I don't remember how it started, I just remember jumping up from the kitchen table where I was doing my homework and pushing past her into the hall. Then her lunging at me and dragging the coat off my back as I made for the front door.

'Don't you dare turn your back on me, Emily Turner. Don't you dare...'

But I'm gone, off, running down the path and into the back lane, grateful for the shelter of its high privet hedge, out into Marchant Street, my breath coming fast, and even though I'm safe now because she rarely leaves the house, I don't stop running until I reach the top of Beach Road and I can smell the sea.

I sit on the seawall and wait for my breath to still, the air salty on my tongue. The tide is going out, leaving its mark on the sand. It's early evening and the sky already leaning to dusk, the end of summer, the autumn term. I think about my homework sitting on the kitchen table and what excuse I can give tomorrow. I'm always the first to hand my homework in. I never go out at night, I'm not allowed. I used to think it would be different when I reached seventeen but if anything, she tightened her grip. She wanted us to do more together, 'like mothers and daughters do,' she said. She'd bought me a calorie counting wheel, insisting we both needed to lose weight. A diet would be good for us.

I feel in my jeans pocket in the hope of finding some loose change, enough for a packet of chips from the chippy, but all I come up with are crumpled tissues and an old, sticky boiled sweet. I put the sweet in my mouth. I'll make it last. A wind has sprung up and I miss my coat.

I get up off the wall and go down the steps to the shelter of the beach. I'm at home here, safe, looking out on the estuary with the choppy, mud-stirred brown water we call, 'the sea' and beyond to the island, to Cloud Island. Which to be honest is not its real name but the name I gave it, and which seems like the right name to me when you see it, as I often do, floating in a sea fret.

I walk along the beach looking for twin shells the colour of fingernails, half-sunk in the wet sand. I collect them. It started when I was small and I believed they were a sign that I was meant to be one of a pair, a twin. Surely, I wasn't meant to do this alone. Where was my brother or sister?

I'm bending down to excavate a shell when I hear a wild screeching above me. I stop and look up into the sky at a flock of gulls mobbing a lone heron. I feel the heron's heart beating fast in its grey feathered chest, just as mine had as

I'd run from the house. I find a stick among the seaweed and launch it into the sky hoping to scatter the gulls. But they are way beyond reach.

'Good try,' says a voice from behind me.

I turn to see the owner of the voice. I recognise him straight away, though I don't know his name. He catches the school bus most days, only he doesn't go to school like us, he's at the art college and he's older, nineteen, maybe even twenty.

'Hi,' I say.

'Hi. Don't worry, it'll fly off home soon. It's the heron from the station pond.'

'How do you know?'

'Arnold, he's the guy who keeps the donkeys. Has a field there. He knows all about the heron. I went down once, took some photos. You collecting shells or something?'

'Not really, just out for a walk.' I rub my hands together and turn my back to the wind as it gusts off the sea.

He turns with me and leans into it. 'You're cold,' he says. He reaches out and touches my arm. My pulse quickens, his gentleness like an ambush.

'I'm fine,' I say.

'Got a coat you can borrow, probably a bit big, but it's warm. It's up there in the van.' He nods towards the seafront. 'I'll get it for you. I need to fetch my rucksack anyway.'

'No need,' I say, 'I'll be OK. I'll have to be going home soon.'

'No trouble, you can give it back to me on the bus. Wait here.'

Before I can argue he breaks into a run across the beach, his long legs eating up the distance. I watch him take the steps two at a time then disappear. Above me, the gulls disperse and the heron flies off. In no time he's back, barely out of breath and armed with coat and rucksack.

'There you go,' he drapes a heavy green parka over my shoulders. It smells of paint and oranges. I push my arms in the sleeves and zip it up.

'Thanks,' I say. 'You're Jessica's brother, aren't you? Sorry, I don't know your name.'

'It's Finn,' he says, 'and you're Emily, yeh?'

I nod, feel my face flush at the mention of my name. He knows who I am. He looks at me. I don't turn away. His eyes are an inky blue, like the mussel shells that hang on the breakwater.

'I'm going down to the dunes to light a fire. I've got the gear in here.' He pats the rucksack on his back. 'Got a couple of cans and a sandwich. Come if you like,' he says.

I hesitate. If I don't go back soon before it gets dark who knows what trouble there'll be. But this, this here and now of quiet voices, and warm coats, of wind, sea and sky, is where I want to be. I nod. 'Cool,' I say.

We walk along the beach, following the tracks of seabirds and dogs, under the pier, past the ruin of the old marine lake. Finn whistles songs I don't know and trails a stick that makes a furrow behind us. Mostly we walk in silence, until we reach the dunes.

'This'll do, here,' he says throwing his rucksack down in the marram grass at the dune's edge by a small circle of stones and ash. 'I've brought sticks, but we'll need some driftwood.' He squats down to pick out the charred remnants of a previous fire and begins to unpack his rucksack.

I forage for dry wood on the strandline among the black pods of kelp and the tangle of fishing rope and plastic waste. In no time the fire is lit, and we sit warming our hands, backs to the dunes, looking out to sea. Finn passes me a can, prises open the lid on his sandwich box and offers me a cheese and pickle sandwich. When I finish eating, I pull the ring on my can and suck at the beery froth that bubbles up. I look out beyond the flames to the shadowy mud flats left by the retreating tide and to the foraging birds. The light is leaving the sky and the island sits like a blue whale in the throat of the estuary.

'Ever been out there?' asks Finn, 'to the island, I mean.'

'No never. Why, have you?'

'Once. My uncle, Thatcher's got a boat and he took us. It's quite something when you get up close, those cliffs are big and it's not easy to find somewhere to land, the beaches are all pebble.'

'I'd like to, one day, at least I think I would but...'

'But what?'

'You'll think I'm mad but since I was a kid, I've always thought of it as magical, in a good way, you know, like an enchanted island. I called it Cloud Island because it just sits there floating above the sea. It's unreal. I guess I'm not sure I want to break the spell. I used to think one day I'll swim there, escape to the island, pick the wild peonies and live off the land. I'll look back from there to here and know I'm a million miles away and out of reach.'

'Except you could be reached, by boat.'

'True, but I was just a kid then. And it was just a fantasy.'

'I don't think you're allowed to pick the peonies either. They're pretty rare.'

'I know,' I say. 'I'd like to see them though.'

'I can take you sometime, if you like. They come out in May.'

Finn turns towards me, his face amber, gentle in the firelight. 'Can I take your picture?' He lifts a camera, a proper camera with a strap that goes around his neck, from his rucksack. 'OK?'

I smile and nod and do my best to avoid the lens. But after a while I forget. I get used to the click of the shutter, to the camera's gaze, to Finn taking pictures of everything, not just me. I feed the fire with driftwood, poke about in its ashes, watch the flames and smoke curl away into the night.

When he finishes, he puts the camera back into the rucksack. 'Cool,' he says, sitting down so close to me our arms touch. He smells of woodsmoke and paint and oranges and I don't want him to move. 'You'll have to see them. Come by the house tomorrow night, I'll have them developed by then.'

'I'm not sure I can, getting out isn't always easy.'

'You're out now.'

'I know but I'm not supposed to be.'

'You're seventeen, aren't you?'

'You don't know my mother.'

'Well, I'll come by and pick you up in the van, if that helps.'

I sigh, 'I'm not sure it does but thanks.'

We sit in silence looking into the fire. There is no mistaking the weight of his arm against mine. He reaches over and trails a finger down my cheek, loops a strand of hair behind my ear. My heart is in my mouth. He leans into me. I turn to him and our lips meet in a soft, fire-lit kiss. The air around me crackles. My heart is a full moon rising over the island. My hopes are the stars coming out. And I pray Finn won't stop.

Through the gaps in the privet, I see the kitchen light and I know she's waiting. How dare I stay out so late? I am cruel and heartless making her suffer like this. Where did I get that coat? Are those love bites on my neck? She claws at my clothes. When I resist, she raises her hand and slaps me hard across the face because it's what I deserve, worrying her like that. 'Say something,' she screams. My silence only makes it worse.

126

But I have swallowed my words. It is summer and I am far away on a pebble beach at the edge of the tide, behind me the cliffs and in my hands a bunch of wild peonies.

The Shape of You

Parveen's heels tap on the boards as she paces the studio. 'What are you afraid of?' she says. 'Our old friends are all gone now, I shouldn't wonder. So you see, it will just be us. And you need a holiday. You can't work all day and night in this damn studio.'

'Why not?' says Tess, putting down a maquette and rubbing her hands on an ancient cloth.

'Because. That is why not. Because you've got circles like black moons under your eyes and your complexion is as white as these ghosts you are afraid of. You need a holiday.'

'I don't know why you call them ghosts.'

'Well, the tsunami for one thing, or have you forgotten?'

'But not there, it was the fishing villages that suffered the worst.'

'Well, all the more reason to go then. We may meet up with old friends. I can book our flights. Auntie's house is waiting.'

'But my work,' says Tess.

'It's a holiday. You don't take holidays now? It will do you good,' says Parveen.

'Perhaps,' says Tess.

'What is your problem? How often have I heard you say one day, one day you will go back?'

'But it was all a long time ago.'

'What is bothering you Tess? If I didn't know better, I would think you are still in love and not just with India.'

Parveen stands back, folds her arms and looks hard at Tess. She smiles, 'That's it, you are still in love.'

'Nonsense,' says Tess.

The studio is Tess's white space, her sea, brick and floor the colour of eggshell. The air is imprinted with a musk of salt and spice, in the corner an old easy chair covered with a pale, yellow throw where she sometimes sleeps. On the bench by her drawing board, a litter of tools, papers, books. A couple of plinths, remnants of her work: friezes, unfinished heads and discarded figures inhabit the place along with a fine layer of plaster dust. She has been working in plaster, always she returns to it.

Barun's first love had been stucco, the kind that adorned the temples of Kanchipuram. But his father insisted he work in stone. It was his birthright. They were all stone masons in that town, working as much by instinct as by education. 'A stone without cracks will sing,' Barun said. 'It will sing you its song as you work, uncovering itself. It is never predictable only there to be chosen. The master knows when he has the stone worth shaping.'

You were chola, dark skin, warm blood back from the well, then bucket, soap, lather, water, swilling away the granite dust, smelling of cardamom and sandalwood. I waited for you in my room in the Mamalla Bhavan where we smoked our Kerala grass and made love under the ancient ceiling fan. I was Radha to your Krishna. It is impossible, you said to sculpt stone that is not yours and yet if I close my eyes, I can still feel the shape of you beneath my hands.

In the morning, Tess leaves the studio for her flat where she showers, dries her hair and rubs oil into her hands. She dresses in black trousers and shirt, mindful of the interview later that day. On her way back she buys coffee, croissant, a ripe mango, and three different cheeses.

A thin sunbeam filters through the trees and patterns the window glass and studio floor. Tess makes coffee, grabs a croissant. Then sitting at her drawing books, she begins to sketch: waves, fish, underwater creatures with arms stretched, hair streaming like the Ganges, eyeless gods and goddesses, an empty shore, the sole remaining temple, each image morphing into the next devouring the white page.

'What are you doing?' says Parveen.

'Just sketching,' says Tess.

'Well,' says Parveen, going over to a step ladder and dumping her bag on its bottom rung. 'I've been busy, booking our flights. It's all done. So don't bother arguing. Sadly, we cannot stay in Auntie's house after all. It is let now, an impossibly good rent, but I will find us an excellent hotel with a pool of course.' Parveen peers over Tess's shoulder at the sketch book. 'Shouldn't you finish the head you were working on before the BBC come. When is it they are coming?'

'Today, four thirty.'

'Ah, so that is why you are dressed up. Do you think they'll ask you why you work in plaster? They usually do. What will you say?'

'I don't know. I'll make something up.'

'What is this you are drawing? Very watery. Oh look, the shore temple. So you *have* been thinking of going back.'

'I'm not sure I have much choice, do I?'

'Don't pretend you aren't excited.'

'You're the one who thinks it's such a good idea.'

'Just imagine, no one will bother you there. No BBC, no dealers, we will be tourists, nothing more. Whose face is that? There.' Parveen points to a face between a swimming monkey and a temple roof.

130

Tess shrugs her shoulders.

'OMG, it is him. Barun. You are drawing your lost lover.'

'Now you're being ridiculous,' says Tess

'*Plus ça change*,' says Parveen, pointing at the decorated elephant being led down the opposite side of the dual carriageway.

'Nothing and everything,' says Tess taking in the traffic, the concrete and the smog laden sky hanging over the city.

'There are still black kites,' says Parveen looking out of the taxi windows to the birds wheeling overhead.

'But not vultures. They are dying out, by all accounts.'

'They were never my favourite,' says Parveen. 'Quite ugly, in fact.'

'On a pile of bones maybe. But see them soar, then they are handsome.'

'You have the strangest way of looking at things.'

When Tess wakes, it's dark outside and the lights have come on around the hotel pool. Parveen is still asleep. Tess orders pancakes and curd with fresh bananas and tea from room service and stands on the balcony outside, waiting for the delivery.

Every morning in the canteen at the Mamalla Bhavan I ate banana and curd. I was alone by then. Parveen would not stay another week. Three months in India had been long enough and besides, she told me I was kidding myself if I thought anything would come of it. The marriage was arranged and such a thing could never be undone she said. Fuck you, I said. I thought of leaving with her then, but it was a thought as fleeting as the glimpse into a sitter's soul.

At the hotel pool, fat dragonflies patrol the water and a woman chases leaves with a besom brush.

'Tomorrow we can go shopping in the mall or Spencer

131

Plaza, maybe visit Kapaleeshwar Temple. It is number one thing to do on Trip Advisor. What do you say?'

Tess has no desire to go shopping but nods her agreement all the same.

'I think I'll book a manicure here at the spa,' says Parveen 'Maybe henna. Shall I book for you? We will be like young brides.'

How I'd envied Barun's bride-to-be, Lina. She would have her hands and feet adorned in mehndi for the wedding. I'd tried not to think of it. In the mornings I went to the Shore Temple beach where the women sold sarees and massages to tourists. When they had no takers, they would come and sit by me, smoke a beedi and chew their betel. Once they hennaed my hands and draped my head in a Kashmiri shawl. 'Dulhan,' they cried then laughed open-mouthed, their gold-capped teeth glinting in the sun. But I was no bride.

Tess books into the Sunrise Guest House with its painted roof terrace and a view across the Bay of Bengal. She emails Parveen to tell her she's sorry. She hadn't planned to leave but she has to see if Barun is still here, by the shore. She will only be staying for one night, maybe two, and not to worry. The chip-chip percussion of a thousand masons' chisels and hammers call to her and it doesn't take her long to find the address she is looking for. She fixes a taxi for the morning then wanders the town and the shore until dusk. The sun falls in a breath, liquefying the horizon, silhouetting the temple, sole survivor of a lost civilisation. Did he see it before the wave? Was he there when the sea gave up its secrets, drawing back to reveal the seven sacred temple ruins?

The bungalow has a wide verandah. It sits low in a garden of hibiscus and frangipani, among lawns overhung by coconut palm and banana. The faint hiss of a sprinkler greets Tess as she steps out of the taxi onto the gravel. Time hangs in the scented morning air. She walks towards the verandah steps. A woman appears in the shadow of the doorway, a pink saree pallu draped over her head and held across her face. Only her eyes are visible.

'Namaste,' says Tess, putting her hands together in greeting, 'I am here to see Mr. Barun Gurumurthy. I am an old friend. My name is Tess.'

The woman hesitates, looks hard at Tess but then nods, 'Follow me,' she says.

The door to the workshop is open and even though he is crouched down with his back to them, even though his hair is white and does not curl at his neck and his arms are no longer those of a young man, Tess knows it's Barun. The woman stoops and whispers in the sculptor's ear. Barun freezes, his shoulders slump, he stops what he is doing and slowly, very slowly he puts his chisel down. Then he stands and he turns to face Tess. He is looking at her, but his eyes do not meet hers. They wander skyward, flit, unable to settle. His eyes have become the lotus leaves of the stone gods, sculpted blank.

'Tess?' He says and he holds out a hand.

She steps forward to take it in hers. 'Barun, yes, it's me. Tess.'

'It's not possible. I am dreaming.' He is gripping her hand tight now. 'Is it? Is it you? Tess? After all this time.'

'After all this time, yes. Look.' She takes his hand and lays it on her face. Barun's fingers trace her cheekbones, lips, eyes, forehead. He smiles. 'See, it is me.' She whispers. She closes her eyes. Time draws them back like the wave.

He pulls her to him. Their arms are around each other. They are laughing. They stand and sway as if in danger of falling. Their faces are wet with tears.

'How did it happen?' asks Parveen.

'The stone, they think, chippings lodged in his eyes. An occupational hazard.'

'It is a tragedy,' says Parveen.

'I suppose there are worse things,' says Tess. 'He is still working, he has his hands, he is still Barun.'

'Worse things? You mean the wave?'

'Who would have thought Lina would die in the tsunami? I was sure it must be her, there in the doorway but I'd forgotten Barun had a sister. Two in fact, and both survived. You know what scares me the most? Not the wave or the drowning. It's before that, it's the sea draining away, retreating, leaving the shore, empty, blank. That's the worst of it. Losing the sea. It isn't supposed to be like that.'

'Lina would have seen it all,' says Parveen.

'Perhaps she saw the temples. Barun says the fishermen saw them that day, the seven pagodas, covered in barnacles and mud,' Tess sighs.

Parveen reaches out and places her hand over Tess's. 'What say we go shopping tomorrow? But only if you like.'

'Shopping? OK. Why not? Tomorrow, we will go shopping,' says Tess, already knowing the shape of what she will make. Of a woman half-seen, a man sculpting stone, eyes like lotus leaves, feet encrusted in barnacles and mud.

What is There to Cry About Today?

She steps outside to breathe the bite of winter air and rid herself of the hum of death. In the yard, ice holds fast to the puddles and the saucers of cats' milk. She takes the saucers inside to the kitchen, holds them under the hot tap until the ice cracks and splinters like glass into the sink, then puts down fresh and stands scanning the track waiting for the doctor's car. That's when Mira sees them: on a late, winter afternoon, as shadows gather in the corners of the hay barn and blackbirds hide in the hawthorn. They come the day her father dies, flying above Black's Farm, while he lies cooling in his bed. They come at dusk, out of a sky beaded red and grazed raw by the sun.

As they fly above her she counts seven, seven long necked swans, like black arrows flying over Paradise along the river in the direction of the Nature Reserve. She wonders who is there; if he is there? It's Fergus Wilde she's thinking of with his dark hair and his bony face. But then she thinks, even if he is, she won't stay anyway, now it's over. One night and she'll be gone, out of this place for good and back in the real world.

It's been eleven years since they were sixteen and still he comes to her. It doesn't matter who Mira is with. Take her current boyfriend Darren, as a case in point, they've been together three years, they practically live together in Darren's north London flat but it makes no difference, Fergus is always there, sometimes in the day, always at night, blurring the boundaries between waking and dreaming. And it doesn't matter where she is; the summer spent in the south of France, the winter teaching in Luxor, Fergus is there. She cannot escape him. Fergus eats miles and flies continents.

It's three o'clock when she puts her coat on, the day after her father's funeral and her brothers, John and Mattie are out feeding the ewes. The Reserve is barely a mile and half from the farm but she hasn't been there since that day. The day they set off, shouting their goodbyes, loaded down with picnic food, swim gear, plastic shoes for plodging in the river, a stash of dope, a packet of Lambert and Butlers and a couple of bottles of stolen wine. The day they came back in silence. Mira thinks, if she's right, she'll be there in time to see the swans.

The track is edged with low walls of sullied snow that have turned to ice, refusing to give up. The wind is growing from the east. She is reminded how she hates it, this possessing, unrelenting cold; cannot get used to it. If she's not careful Mira thinks, if she stays too long it will steal her senses and scour the colour from her life, like it does the land, reducing everything, sheep, wood, and fields, to stone. But she needn't worry. She's done her bit, she's done what they wanted, looked after her father and now another life is waiting, a new term and new students.

Fergus Wilde puts the kettle on the gas stove. He warms his hands and waits for it to boil. He's been out repairing the door in the northern hide. It's the furthest from the path and the central lake. It overlooks the brown, mineral rich, river and occasionally he sees kingfishers here, shooting up river across the shallow fast flowing water. He doesn't mind the kingfishers, they're good looking, not like the ducks who are too noisy and the herons, too much like miserable old men. Lately he's grown to admire the swans. He read somewhere that swans pair for life. They only *divorce when there is a nesting failure*. It made him think of his parents. He supposed you could describe what happened eleven years ago as *a nesting failure,* but something much worse than divorce.

Most days Fergus wonders what he's doing at the Reserve, why he came back. Most days he concludes he doesn't want to think about it and he's getting out anyway. As soon as he can find something he'll be out. A friend of Jonty's, bird mad just like Jonty, has promised to get him work on the new building site in town when the weather changes. But deep down Fergus knows that when the time comes leaving will be hard, because here is home. He looks at the clock. They'll be coming in fifteen, twenty, minutes and they'll be expecting him. He fills a bucket with gnarled potatoes from a sack in the corner of the kitchen, takes the kettle off the stove and puts on his winter gear: padded green coat that lets in the damp, thick wool hat, and thermal gloves, and sets off on the path through the reed beds to the edge of the lake.

Mira's feet crunch the bent straw of reeds at the lakeside. She knows it's Fergus, despite the hat and coat, despite his back being to her. Her mouth is dry

Fergus turns, sensing her. He knows her father has died, in a small place like this you get to know most things quickly. He's been thinking perhaps he will see her but this... this is not what he'd expected.

'Mira,' his heart is in his mouth, falling from his tongue. 'I was sorry...sorry about your father.'

'Thanks.' Mira coughs, looks down and pushes her boots into the half frozen mud. It crackles. 'I've come for the swans,' she says. She looks up at him. The light is changing to copper, thin and liquid, catching the feather tops of the trees. 'I saw them fly over the farm in this direction. I thought someone might be feeding them,' she looks down at the bucket by his feet.

'You're right there. Me,' he says, 'didn't have much choice.' He coughs and she sees his breath like smoke in the air. 'Lost one when the lake first froze, got trapped you know, so I started to check up on the others every day, fed them too and now more come, word travels fast in the world of swans. Iris, do you know her? She lives on the smallholding, a way down the track at the end of Eden Row. Gave me a couple of sacks of potatoes, they seem to like them.' He takes off his hat and shakes his head.

He's got the same thick hair, longer than she remembers. She looks at him, his face is bony, his nose and his lips are both bigger than they should be and something powerful draws her to him just as it did that summer and every night since, and all the times she imagined she saw him in the shadows, at the edge of her vision, heard him whispering that he would love her for ever, that they belonged here, together. Now in the borderlands of the day, with both moon and sun in the sky, Mira feels time shift shape and the ground beneath her slip away...

...Summer. A hot, damsel fly day, the river running slow, speckled with spit and swarming with midges, she sits at the edge of the water, Fergus at her side. They are drying off from swimming, his warm sun-baked skin presses hers, his arm is around her, she is alive with his touch. Before long they will leave the others to go down to the wildflower meadow. Out of sight and stoned, they will kiss and touch each other, never quite daring to go the whole way until now, until this day, the day that Mattie comes to find them. He is running and his face is full of dread. He comes with the news they don't want to hear, that Fergus fears more than his own drowning, and Fergus fears drowning, fears being sucked under the water and never surfacing, more than anything. He has dreamed about it as far back as he can remember. The first dream he ever dreamed, he was drowning and Aaron saved him...

'I'd like to stay and watch, if it's OK?' she says, remembering how Fergus wanted no one, not her, not one of them in the days that followed. How he was lost to her, how he hadn't even looked at her on the day of the funeral and how her prayers had seemed as faint as dandelion seeds in the wind.

He nods, then tips more potatoes at the water's edge. They stand in silence and wait. She listens for the rise of his breath, looks up with him at the sky and sees the swans flying out of the trees and over the North Hide, circling the lake their wings outstretched, black feet hanging. In seconds they are skimming the surface. They swim across, then step out of the water onto the frozen edges and up to Mira and Fergus's feet. They arch their necks downwards to peck at the potatoes.

'I meant to, you know, keep in touch but I couldn't not after...' he says.

'I know,' she says.

'You see...' but he can't finish

'I see.'

...walking back up to the farm, they pushed their bikes, it didn't seem right to be riding. John and Mattie were in front, she was behind.

Her father was first to greet them, appearing out of the hay barn as they reached the yard. 'Oh aye, here she is, here comes our little actress, the drama queen, always crying, so what's the matter now, eh? What've you found to cry about today?'

It was John who silenced him. Told her father what had happened, how Fergus's twin Aaron was dead. It shouldn't have been a surprise. Aaron had been dying for a long time. Only it wasn't meant to be that day, that summer, it was always going to be another.

Fergus and Mira walk back through the Reserve to the cottage. The sky has grown dark and a savage wind rattles the reed beds and the alder copse. Once inside, Fergus throws logs into the wood burner and leaves its blackened glass doors open for her to get warm by. She can hear him in the kitchen, she can smell bread toasting. She looks around. The room is small and barely furnished, the surface of the table cluttered with clothes, books, paper piles, binoculars, breakfast plates, jars of jam, boxes of cereal, bird seed, soap, towel, a black bottle of CK for men.

Fergus's life spreads before her and she thinks of all the clutter and mess she's tried to clean and sort these past weeks at the farm.

He brings mugs of tea and a plate of toast on a tin tray. 'Bit of a mess, I know, still there's just me, never was very tidy.'

'Thanks.' Mira takes the mug of tea and a piece of toast. His sleeves are pushed up and she tries hard not to stare at the pale olive skin of his arms, his hands with their slender fingers, the bones of his wrist. Fergus sits on the other side of the fire and drinks his tea. She wonders why he lives here. She thinks perhaps he's torturing himself, can't leave it behind. 'How come you're here?' she asks.

'A job,' he says, then adds, 'besides why not? I like it here. I'm part of it, born to it and it makes no difference where I am. I went to India for a while, after you left. I suppose I was running away but it didn't take long before I saw that I didn't want to forget. I didn't need to.'

'I'm sorry,' she says, 'sorry you were with me, not him that day.'

'Don't be,' says Fergus, 'I'm not.' He smiles and looks up at her and thinks she's the same but different. He thinks if anything she's more beautiful than she was then and he wonders how he can let her go again. 'Anyway tell me about you, about teaching, London. I want to hear it all.' So she tells him and when she finishes he says, 'You did the right thing getting away. It has a way of holding onto you this place, of not letting go.'

Mira imagines them together, holding on, Fergus's long arms wrapped round her tight. She sighs. 'I should be getting back,' she says 'I need to pack, I'm catching an early train in the morning.'

'It's a wild night. I'll take you in the pick-up,' says Fergus already on his feet.

She sits next to him in the diesel fuelled air, the nearest she's been to Fergus Wilde in eleven years. Her skin prickles with proximity and she feels the atoms spin in the nest around them. Fergus drives too fast up the rough track to the farm so that their bodies jolt and jump and she is thrown onto him. She cries out and they both laugh, suddenly they are back there in the heat of that summer meadow with their lives stretching in front of them. Then they are silent as Fergus pulls up and stops in front of the gate to the yard.

Mira opens the door of the pick–up, holds on to the handle and turns to him. He looks past her to another place. 'Stay in touch,' she says as she steps down into the fierce wind. He says nothing, just sits unmoving, hunched like a kestrel on a post, eyes fixed on its prey. She feels him watching her as she opens and closes the gate, then crosses the yard, his eyes drilling into her back. Only as she shuts the farmhouse door does she hear the engine start up.

John and Mattie are watching the six o'clock news and

drinking beer. The kitchen is warm and Mira pours herself a whiskey. She puts it to her lips and shudders, she tastes the night she left. She tastes the longing not to go and her mother's insistence on a better life. She tastes the despair and the way she willed him to come. And then she tastes the bottle, how she drank the best part of it and how she waited for him through that long, dreamless night.

A black, northern sky sprawls over the trees and cemetery beyond the farm. Mira dresses for bed, winter pyjamas, bed socks, dressing gown. She carries two hot water bottles with her into her room where the wind screams through the thin, aluminium frames. From the window, only the cold-bred scots pine are visible, swaying in the bucket of dark. She draws the curtains and burrows under the duvet and the frayed Durham quilt. She thinks of Fergus Wilde and the way he smells of that black bottle scent and of grass and river, and she drifts into the deep water between waking and sleeping, her body growing heavy, unmoving.

Mira wakes in the middle of the night struggling for breath. She pushes the quilt from the bed. She's hot suddenly and the air around her is clotted, too thick to breathe. She can smell the lake and hear the beating of wings, like the sails of a thousand feluccas turning in the breeze. A wild drumming throbs around her and the room fills with a rush of spinning wind and the wind is not like the savage wind from the north with its fingers of ice forcing a retreat. No. This is a tropical wind, soft and warm blooded, with velvet fingers.

A pair of arched wings hang above her, obliterating the night. They are all she can see. She counts their spines and their feathers beaded with droplets of water, watches them come ever closer until she feels the coolness of the cob's neck lying in the divide between her breasts. Its head rests

142

on her shoulder and its beak whispers at her ear. Its damp, white feathered body, smells of black bottle scent and grass as it presses down on her and she feels its wild pulsating heart.

Mira sleeps late. When she gets up she pushes back the curtains and looks out on to fields made green by sunlight and a winter blue sky. She sees the snow at the edges of the track beginning to disappear. Downstairs, she searches for a clean cup among the remains of breakfast that litter the kitchen table: the egg stained plates, half eaten toast, last night's whiskey glass.

In the yard puddles of ice are melting. Mira puts down morning milk for the cats and stands back in the lee of the doorway out of the wind, so that the pale sun warms her. She drinks her coffee and watches the cats appear from the barn and run over to where the saucers sit. Their long shadows dance in the morning light and their pale tongues lap at the saucers until their whiskers drip with milk.

Sateen Goose Tail

The Eye is unblinking, stretching across the river in an arc of steel. Ellen runs her fingers back and forth over the fabric, feeling the uneven surface, following the delicate lines of stitching that give shape to a thousand small cushions. From the window she watches the Eye turn an iridescent green against an afternoon sky already streaked with red. Pedestrians crossing the bridge stoop against the late March cold. Snow still threatens in the North. Spring is elusive. Ellen longs for the end of a month whose coming haunts her, a cruel reminder of what is stitched in her heart.

Behind her, quilts lie in their racks, wrapped in tyvek, rolled on cardboard, tagged and dated. They hang mummified in a temperature of fifty-five degrees, plus or minus five. Rolled not folded. For a quilt should never be folded lest it crease and mark although all the quilts she'd ever known, especially those made by her grandmother Alice, had been folded at some time or another, like the *Medallion* they'd buried her in. As far as Ellen remembered it hadn't been a question of which clothes, but which quilt, and how to make sure Alice's head lay at the centre of the eight-pointed star. There were times Ellen felt sure her grandmother was looking down on her from above, a star with a face, rouged cheeks and black pennies for eyes.

They'd sewn the *Double Wedding Ring*, a grandmother and granddaughter working together, threading their smooth coated *betweens*, Ellen's with a slightly larger eye, long into the evening when it was really too dark to sew but they could not bring themselves to stop. There was hardly a woman in the Avenue who hadn't come for that quilt: Deborah Forrester after her first child, the girl who worked in the University Library, Emma – it hadn't worked for her, Nancy and Vicky – both had sworn by it. It was the quilt Ellen's twins had been conceived under. But its edges were frayed now, its bindings unravelling. It was in need of replacing.

This *Sateen Goose Tail* is exactly what she needs. It's in fine condition, feathers full and round and stitched with a thread run through beeswax. It has most likely never been washed. Its provenance is unknown but there's no mistaking a North Country quilt.

Ellen waits until she's alone, then lifts the quilt from the open drawer and folds it to fit into her rucksack. She pushes it down making sure it's hidden, then makes her way to the marble hall and the reception desk. She says goodnight to Molly the receptionist and leaves the Museum for the last time. She crosses the river on the Eye and walks up into the city to catch the Metro home. In the darkening sky above, her grandmother's star hovers and winks at her.

Every day Ellen is mindful that the police might come. That they will arrive in the Avenue, their blue lights flashing for all the neighbours to see. They will step up to her door, ring the bell and that will be that. She will deny it of course. Her husband, Richard, will be outraged. But they will charge her and who knows what might happen then. She does her best not to dwell on it.

On the first day of April, Ellen lifts the quilt from the linen chest and lays it on the bed. She unwraps it slowly from its layers of tissue and muslin. She closes her eyes and smoothes her palms across its rippled surface like a swan's wing, a baby's skin, virgin snow, the quilt is flawless like her child had been. It's no April Fool but exactly what Mira needs now that she's decided to stay.

Ellen knows what it is to lose a child, Aaron the first born of the twins gone at fifteen. Now this grandchild of hers, Mira's baby, barely conceived before it was over, gone too, a fragile bubble of life that faltered and burst. No wonder Fergus, the second born had fled, but she knows him, he'll be back. He can smooch off all he likes to live in an apartment, in a high rise named Riverview where there's no river to be seen for miles around, but he'll be back. Ellen sighs. Sometimes Fergus doesn't have the sense he's born with. About the most sense he'd ever shown was in finding Mira.

She folds the wrapping back around the quilt and puts it into the suitcase. 'I'm off out,' she calls to Richard in his study, but there's no reply. The day is warm, unseasonably so. The windows of the house are open and as Ellen approaches, she can hear a radio. Someone is reading Robbie Burns *Ae Fond Kiss*: *fare thee weel thou first and fairest...* A starling flies out from under the eaves and settles on the fence.

The house has been hollowed out and opened to the sun. Inside, Mira has stripped it back to bare boards and ageing plaster and taken down the thick velvet curtains. From the bedroom window, you can look out across the fields to where the horses graze. You can watch the slow melting of the mists that hang above the river in the early morning. Mira is growing into the place.

She has not, nor ever will, get used to losing her baby. Embryonic or not, it makes no difference. She hears its tiny, spirit voice on the wind, in the cry of the cats that inhabit the garden, the threads of sheep wool that blow on the wire, the rattle of winter reeds. She cannot go back now and leave her spirit child alone. Her home is here now, in these rooms she makes her own.

Mira has stripped back the palimpsest of lives. She has patched plaster and rollered walls in *Bird's Egg, Clouded Sky, White Handkerchief*, filled dishes with sea glass, set candles on trays and wildflowers in preserving jars. She has raided charity shops for pots and pans, for china, for pale violet plates and turquoise teacups, bed linen, kitchen scales, old photographs. She's found unwanted furniture in second-hand shops: a bed, a dresser, a scrubbed kitchen table and two chairs.

Ellen has promised her there will be another child and she believes her. First babies are often lost Ellen says, and sometimes for the best, her loss must not be taken as a bad sign. There were things you could do and Mira was determined to do everything she could. Only yesterday she'd begun to clear the borders of their weeds and brambles and on Ellen's instructions she'd planted a rosemary bush and pulled up the mint.

Mira sees that Ellen is wheeling a suitcase as she approaches the front door. She puts the paint roller in its tray and hurries to open the door.

'Hi, come in,' she says. She looks at the suitcase, 'You OK?'

'Fine, I'm good,' says Ellen, following her into the kitchen and putting the suitcase next to the table.

'Tea?' asks Mira who is already at the sink filling the kettle and drying the tea cups and saucers.

'Lovely.'

'You going somewhere?' Mira puts the cups and saucers on the table.

'No,' Ellen laughs. 'Tried that once but it didn't work,

ended up coming back the next day. No, something I got for you. Bedding stuff.'

'Brilliant,' says Mira, filling the teapot and putting it next to the cups. She fetches milk from a small fridge.

Ellen looks at the kitchen window, 'What about curtains? You'll need some.'

'I'm not really one for curtains,' says Mira, pouring tea into the cups. 'I've got a blind up at the bedroom window and one for the front room. It's all I need for now.'

'It's looking great. I mean it. I envy you, a whole house to yourself. It wasn't something you thought of when I was young. Women didn't have their own room even, well not the women I knew, let alone a house. Now look at you and this place.'

'It's growing on me, that's for sure.' Mira jumps up and takes a biscuit tin from the cupboard. She prises the lid off. 'I forgot, I made these.' She holds out the tin. 'Brownies. I've been baking. Now how domestic is that?'

Ellen smiles and reaches in the tin. If I didn't know better, she thinks, I'd say she was pregnant now, what with all this baking and nesting.

They eat their brownies and drink their tea.

'I planted the rosemary bush you gave me yesterday. I uncovered a couple of old roses and lilac in the border waiting to come out. By the time summer comes you won't know the garden.'

'Has Fergus been?'

'He came last night. He turned up with a bottle of wine. It was his...' Mira hesitates.

'Birthday,' says Ellen.

'Yes. I hardly wanted to say. It's a difficult time I know, I'm sorry. It's hard for him too but we drank the wine.'

'The curse of being a twin.'

'Worse for you.'

148

Ellen drains the last of the tea from her cup and puts it back in its saucer. 'What did I say? I told you it wouldn't be five minutes before he'd be back.'

'You did. I'm not just giving up this place, though. I'm not ready. I've barely started.'

'Why should you? But nothing wrong with a visitor every now and then is there? Don't forget it can be cold in the winter, and through the spring. Which reminds me,' Ellen reaches out for the suitcase, unzips it and lifts the quilt onto the table as Mira clears away the cups. 'For the bed,' she says as she takes the quilt from it tissue wrapping. She unfolds it and the two women hold it out by its four corners.

'It's beautiful,' says Mira. 'Perfect. Where did you find it? Did you make it?'

'Handed down,' says Ellen, 'for a purpose of course. It's not just any old quilt.'

'No?'

'No. It's for a wedding night. It's for...well you know. You can't fail under this. Better than any fertility drug, better than rosemary.'

'Let's put it on now,' says Mira.

They take the quilt upstairs and spread it over Mira's bed.

'Perfect,' says Ellen smoothing it down.

Mira stands back and admires the quilt. 'I think we need a glass of wine to celebrate. Wait here.' She disappears and comes back with two tumblers of cold white wine. She hands one to Ellen. 'Sorry, I haven't got round to wine glasses yet.'

The women take their glasses over to the windowsill and lean on it, sipping wine and watching the crows fly back and forth from field to tree, trailing moss and twigs in their beaks.

'It feels special today,' says Mira. 'Like spring is finally on its way.' She smiles.

'Yes, it does,' says Ellen. 'It finally feels like winter is over.

Now the clocks have gone back the days will soon be long and the nights light so it will barely ever get dark. That's the beauty of the North. And I can babysit for you, you know, if you want, when it happens. You'd never be on your own.'

'I know. Thanks. Let's drink to a new season,' says Mira. 'Then I'll top us up, shame not to finish the bottle.'

'To a new season,' says Ellen raising her glass.

By the time Ellen leaves, it is dusk and her head is as light as her suitcase. For once the wine has made her feel good and mellow, like wine is supposed to. Children are playing out in the street, boys just like Fergus and Aaron. How inseparable they were, until Aaron got sick.

She isn't the only one. She knows other women, plenty of women, who've had to find their own way of meeting the loss visited on them. For her it had been a long crawl through the dark maze of a winter with no light. But Mira's coming has changed that. Mira is her Ariadne. Ellen is emerging from the labyrinth. She feels certain of it, what with Fergus visiting and the quilt. She's certain enough to begin watching the nesting birds and to go looking for wood anemones and bluebells in the Dene.

Ellen is thinking of a child to be, and the new quilt she will make. It will be cotton, organic is best for a new-born, soft, pastel shades, hand-stitched, the thread carefully chosen. She is smiling as she pushes open the gate to the house and looks up to see a light on and Richard standing in the bay. Behind him is a shadow, dark as a bruise. She stops. She looks around her and for the first time notices the empty police car parked on the grass verge. She throws back her head and looks up into a darkening sky. She is there, a first, single star Alice with her black penny eyes, shining like sateen in the evening blue. Ellen pushes open the front door and goes inside.

Tokyo Dreaming

Nathan Ashe knew it would have to be soon. The five-day weather forecast promised showery rain, there would be sunny spells with light winds increasing in intensity on the fourth day. Three days then. He had three days in which he must arrange to see her as if by chance, bump into her in the library, outside the lecture hall, in the bar, somewhere she wouldn't suspect. He'd have to think about what he would need, when to do it and how.

Sumiko Ishikawa stood outside the lecture hall, willing herself in. She knew she must carry on as normal to honour the suffering and the sacrifice, and besides she'd promised her mother and keeping a promise to her mother was about all that was left to her in the circumstances. She summoned up her spirit in a breath and pushed open the double doors to Lecture Theatre One. She was not the last in. Nathan Ashe followed behind her. She held the doors open for him.

He sat next to her. How small her feet were. He daren't look up, daren't nudge or whisper. His problem all over, not knowing what to say or how to start. Martine was the only girl he'd ever really managed to talk to, but then three weeks in she'd started ignoring him and seeing some other jerk in English Lit. He'd followed Martine around for a bit but then realised it was futile and he was behaving like a kid. This time there would be none of that juvenile stuff. He wouldn't get it wrong. He was determined.

The complexities of international banking law seemed

irrelevant. Sukimo's head was full of water and explosion. It was only a lack of money that prevented her from going home, that and the thought that once she got there she might be more of a hindrance than a help. There was her mother to think of too. She was not a woman to cross.

The tsunami of news still held her like a magnet; rolling footage of the coastal inundations playing alongside the plumes of steam rising and rising from the Fukushima reactors. Her parents lived in the suburbs, which was some consolation and according to her mother were carrying on as usual, as she should. Sumiko knew already that other student's families had not fared so well. When she could listen no more she got up and left.

What made her get up and leave like that? He should have spoken to her when he had his chance at the very beginning before the lecture started. He couldn't follow her it would be too suspicious. He'd been deep in dreams of the future when she'd stood up and pushed past him. Now he was trapped in a boring lecture theatre – listening to a lecture he should have been interested in only wasn't – instead of making progress with his plan.

It just never came easy with women, did it? Not for him. Maybe it was growing up with men that did it. There'd been plenty of boys without fathers at school but as far as Nathan could remember he'd been the only one without a mother, except for Peter Franks, and he didn't count because his mother was dead.

Her room smelled of earth and rotting leaves. She closed the window. Some places had a scent that was all their own, like Tokyo. In spring the city smelled of pollen and fish and there was noodle soup and petrol in the wind. Its streets were a laundry of wet and humid air. Sumiko turned from the window and gathered up the dirty clothes from the back of her chair and the floor. She stripped her bed and bundled the washing together then made for the stairs and down to the basement where the giant machines hummed, spewing out warm breath.

Nathan caught the bus into town, had a coffee in Varsity and then went shopping. He was calmer now he'd made his plan, the lecture had been good for something at least. He figured he knew where she'd be this afternoon and by then everything would be ready. Having a plan was a comfort, it made him believe it was all possible. It made him think of himself differently, as a man, like a soldier in a foreign war.

Sumiko imagined herself at home sitting on the tatami watching her mother sew, looking at the grey glass in the sliding doors and beyond to where the sea was sucking the water from the bay, gathering itself in a crescendo of readiness to return and overwhelm the land. The door to the basement laundry clicked open. Sumiko turned. It was no one she knew. She smiled at the girl then got up and went to the washing machine where she watched her clothes stuck fast to the edge of the whining drum. She waited for the spin cycle to finish so that she could lift them out, pull them apart and put them into the drier.

As well as the items he'd bought in town and in the supermarket on his way back, Nathan packed a sharp knife and a white sheet, barely soiled by his standards, taken from his narrow single bed. He would have liked a basket but only had a rucksack and he supposed a rucksack would be less suspicious so that was OK.

The girl had put her washing in then left. Sumiko was alone again. She took her clothes from the drier, smelled their soap-powder heat and folded them with more care than was usual. When she'd finished, the pile was a near perfect rectangle.

Once upstairs, not wanting to disturb the washing, she put it on her desk, bent to bury her nose in it, then straightened up, breathed deeply and went to make noodle soup in the kitchen.

He could see her from his room. He could see the kitchen too. She was in the block opposite, her room one floor lower than his. For a long time he'd tried hard not to look but then this last week he allowed himself, besides she never left the blind up at night or at any time when she might have been half dressed. She was more discrete than that; than most. He understood the need for discretion. He thought he understood what Sumiko might be feeling. After all he knew what it was not to go home.

She was about to sit on her bed and eat her soup when there was a knock on the door. She got up, put the soup on the desk next to her washing and opened the door. It was Nathan Ashe. He had a rucksack on his back.

'Hope I didn't disturb you,' he said, 'just wondered if you wanted to come for a walk? The bluebells are out in the woods now. It's not far.'

'Thanks but I don't think so, I've got work to do. I've got an essay...' her voice trailed away.

'It won't take any time, half an hour no more. Say yes.' He saw her hesitate. 'I'm sorry, about the tsunami,' he said hurriedly.

'Thanks,' Sumiko turned to look at the laundry on the desk. 'You want some soup?'

'I'm not hungry.'

154

'Oh, well.'

'You should see the bluebells,' said Nathan, 'and smell them. Like perfume. The woods are full of them. It's a blue carpet. Half an hour, it won't take any more.' He didn't move.

She picked up her soup bowl, looked down into it and said, 'OK. I'll finish my soup then come and see the bluebells but just half an hour. OK?'

'Half an hour,' Nathan nodded. A wave of heat flushed through his veins and broke on his face.

He walked a step behind her in the woods, admiring her dark glossy hair and her tiny frame.

The woods were a cloud of blue and the wind lifted the sweet hyacinth smell. It wasn't Tokyo.

He wanted her to stop. He wanted to stroke her hair. He didn't know what to say. He talked about international business law, the lecture she'd run away from.

She wanted to get back to her room and her white washing. Get on the internet, talk to her brother on *Skype*. She turned. 'This is far enough I think.'

Now was his chance, he had to seize this moment or else all of the thinking and all of his careful preparation would be wasted. 'There's something I want to show you,' he said, 'five more minutes please. It's a surprise. It's cool.' She didn't seem convinced. 'It's just out of the wood and along the lane, through into the gardens, a secret way in. Five minutes.'

'Five minutes no more, then I need to get back. I must...' Her voice wavered. Images of the wave resurfaced and fear coated her tongue.

He was in front of her when they left the wood. She followed him along the lane but he slipped behind her as they reached the gap in the hedge. 'It's here. Step through the gap. Now. Wait.' She stepped through and he put his hands up to her head and covered her eyes. 'Trust me,' said Nathan Ashe, 'just a few more steps forward. Just a few.'

'Don't,' said Sumiko. 'Don't. Please.' The wave was towering and black. He took his hands away from her eyes and she held her breath.

Nathan chose one of the six, slate-topped curved benches that lined the circle and lifted his rucksack off his back. Sumiko watched. Inside the circle there was nothing to see but cherry trees and every tree in blossom, petals lifting on the wind and falling like spring snow. He folded the white sheet into a picnic cloth and put out the food: bread, salt crackers, cheese, prawns, spring onions, tomatoes, sushi, a bottle of soy sauce, two plates and the knife, he'd forgotten forks.

Damn, he should have brought chopsticks. How could he have overlooked it? Now they would have to eat with their fingers. He hoped that wouldn't spoil things. There was nothing he could do, it was too late now. But Sumiko didn't seem to mind. No, Sumiko stood motionless looking up into a cloud of blossom and then back at him. Sumiko was smiling at him. She was standing next to him smiling, and there was cherry blossom in her hair.

this One Wild Place

To Begin – April 2020

The bay fills with water, a spring tide drawn in by the full moon. I smell the salt on the wind that whispers through the house. I watch the moon from my window and wait for my father, Tom, to return. He needs to think, he says, and the sea helps. He is down in the bay walking at the edge of the tide. He is looking out over dark moonlit water, but he is thinking of hills. I am sure of it. His mind is already made up. For days now he's been saying that he should have gone back sooner to help them, that it might have made a difference, and that now it's too late.

I hear him come in, lock the back door behind him, take off his coat and boots. He climbs the stairs and stands in my bedroom doorway, leaning against the frame. I know what he's going to say by the way he's avoiding my gaze, by the way he's looking down at his feet. I know there's no point in resisting.

'I've made up my mind. I'm sorry but we have to go Lila,' he says. 'I don't care about the rules. I can't just leave the farm empty, not now. Besides there are the sheep to think of, what will happen to them? We'll come back, as soon as it's all sorted. I promise. It's my duty. I can't just abandon it and let it all go to ruin.'

I picture the farm, overgrown with ivy and mountain ash, sparrows nesting in the roof, broken windows, a ragwort garden. I see the owls haunting its sills, gatekeepers to a feral world of fox and vole, a world that was once mine, every summer as far back as I can remember.

'Just a few weeks,' Tom says, 'there's nothing to lose, then we'll see.'

See what? I wonder. See how everything has turned upside down, how nothing is the same? See how I've had to say goodbye to my best friends Sophie and Liam? How they sneaked out of quarantine to meet me on the beach the night of my birthday. How we lit a fire in the salty breeze and drank our last tins, watching the flames scallop the night, listening to the gulls crying far away out at sea. See how I was tired of losing and waiting.

I waited forever for my mother, Beth, to come back. Because that's what you do when you're eight and grief clings to you like a coat made for someone else, a coat so big and heavy you can't breathe when you put it on. A coat you cannot take off. And a funeral means nothing. You don't want a mother who's a star roaming untethered in the night sky, or a box of dust or ashes to scatter at the wind. You don't want a memory book.

You long for the mother whose smell and touch and voice you know. You make lists in your head, the list of you and her: hands clasped tight, silver rings on fingers, flip-flops and sun hats, making sandcastles on the beach, sunlight on water, rain and snow, her yellow skirt, red lipstick and high heels, behind the driving wheel, bedtime, *Where The Wild Things Are*, hair fanned on the pillow next to yours, the whisper of her song as you fall asleep...

I take the table of tides from under my pillow and slip it into my rucksack along with a photo of my mother, Beth, and another of my grandparents, Sheila and Mattie on the farm. It is on a blue dusk in early spring, three days after my fifteenth birthday, that we drive out of the West. Turning our backs on the old pier and the soft suck of the incoming tide, we head for the North.

The hills steal up on us after dark when the motorway empties and the comfort blanket of flatlands and warm wind floats off and rears up into barren hills and the glint of a sheep's eye in headlights. Have the sheep survived? And what about Mattie's dog, Dylan? Where is he?

As Tom drives through the night, I make a list to keep us safe: willow and catkin, the shape of trees, blotting paper skies, shooting stars, grey seas, books, school – sometimes, art with Mr. Parry, phone most times, TikTok, FaceTime, Insta, the table of tides, shells, old clothes, red socks, dogs, Tom with his hood up, Mattie's handkerchief...

When I was very small, I was afraid of the dark, so Mattie wrapped the dark up to keep me safe and put it away in his big handkerchief that smelled of sheep's wool. Now high in the wild hills, where the world finally flattens out to heather and fell, the dark has taken him, and I'm afraid again.

I wake late. A pale, fragile sun shines through the thin curtains. I'm back in a childhood summer; the rose trellis wallpaper, sloping ceiling and the familiar softness of the quilt under my fingers. But it's not summer. It's spring, and there is no Sheila and no Mattie, but everywhere reminders that they're gone. I don't want to be here without them. I close my eyes and think of home; out on the salt marsh with Sophie, poking at the small white ghost crabs in muddy pools, lying in the sun on the riverbank waiting for the salty lick of the tide to flood the estuary, water like glass.

Loss like stone, I swallow hard, climb out of bed, pull on my jeans and sweatshirt and fasten back my hair. From downstairs the smell of burnt toast wafts up along with the sound of the radio. I look out of the window in the hope that Dylan will be there, below in the yard, but nothing.

Tom is in the kitchen frying eggs. He turns off the radio. He's taken to doing it whenever I come into the room. When I asked why, although it was obvious to anyone with half a brain, he told me there was too much news, best to ration it. There's toast and tea on the kitchen table by the window.

'No butter. I forgot to bring any,' Tom says.

'Marmalade? Jam?' I ask. He shakes his head.

I sit on the bench at the table and look out from the wide kitchen window to Sheila's garden. Beyond it the sky is hazy, clouds have gathered after an early sun. Across the valley the fields and far hills are blue, the colour of distance, of absence, of the place you can never reach. It looks like rain.

Tom puts a plate of eggs in front of me. 'Sleep OK?' Then before I can answer, 'I'm off to mend the fence in the top field with Bryan. He's here now, by the sound of it. Don't worry I'll be careful. Better be off. You could start sorting out Sheila's things if you like.'

'Don't forget to ask Bryan about Dylan, Dad. Please,' I call out, as Tom grabs a coat and wellies and makes for the back door.

All journey I'd been thinking of Dylan, imagining how, when I stepped from the car, he would be there to greet me. How I would ruffle my hands in his thick coat, put my nose to his and say hello. Always before, when we pulled into the yard, often late at night, Dylan would come out and stand patiently at Mattie's feet until Tom lifted me half asleep from the car, took me inside and put me down in the chair by the Aga. Dylan would let rip then, barking and chasing his tail round and round, like some crazy dog, jumping up and licking my face.

But last night there was no such greeting. I'd stood at the door and called and called, but nothing. I'd taken the torch and checked Mattie's old shed, the hay barn and the field below the garden, but there was no sign of Dylan anywhere.

The catch is broken and the handle missing on Sheila's small, cream vanity case. I lift it out from under the bed and lay it on top of the quilt. Inside is a tangle of coloured beads and cheap necklaces and beneath them the ring box. In it is the sapphire ring that Sheila said would one day be mine. I open the box and slip the ring onto my left middle finger, but it's too big and trying it on feels all wrong, like Beth's rings, like the mess of beads and chains that will take forever to unravel. I put the ring back in the box, close the lid of the case and push it back under the bed. Enough. I'm not sure I should even be in Sheila and Mattie's room and besides I need to find Dylan.

I put on my coat and boots, grab an old pair of gloves that smell of lavender, too big but I have none of my own, open the door and step outside. The air is mild but there's no salty sting or rising gull, instead it's hills. Hills above and hills below, hills across on the other side of the valley. Hills and sky meeting in cloud and the first spots of rain in the wind. It can be savage, the weather here. Today it's not so bad, today it's misty and damp and the air holds me in the soft fold of its wings.

I push the gloves down in my coat pockets and make my way through Sheila's garden to the gate and out, following the dry-stone wall and the old track down across the fields. When I reach the stile, I take the footpath that leads to the cemetery and on through the churchyard. I stop and look for Sheila's robin, like we always did. According to her it arrived when I was born. There's no sign of the robin today so I make my way to a cluster of grey stone terraced houses and shops, out into the main street.

The shops are mostly shut apart from the small Co-op

and the chemist. The place is deserted, it feels desolate and now I'm not even sure why I've come, just that I always came with Sheila for coffee and chocolate cake. I stop at the window of the tea shop and peer inside. Nothing. I'm about to go into the Co-op and buy some bread and milk, maybe a couple of tins, because we have to eat something, when a voice calls out from across the street.

'Lila. Hey, Lila. Is that you? It is you. What the f...?'

I smile and turn. I'd know that voice anywhere. Connor, there's no mistaking him, except he looks taller than he did two summers ago, and he was tall enough then. His friends Jo-jo, and Maeve from the caravan site, who I'd met by the river and hung out with that summer, called him, 'The Hulk.'

Connor Greaves, legs like fossil trees, shoulders and chest bursting out of his Newcastle United football shirt, curly hair, smile as wide as a barn door, and beside him at his feet, a dog on a rope. A dog that from where I'm standing looks suspiciously like Dylan.

My stomach flips, I smile, wave, hurry across the street. I look down at the dog. But it's not Dylan. Its face is longer than Dylan's and it doesn't have that funny shaped patch of white that Dylan has over his left eye.

Connor goes to put his arms round me in a loose kind of bear hug. He's grown all right but so have I. I'm nearly as tall as him. He steps away. 'Fuck, sorry, keep forgetting.' He stands back. 'Well fancy, long time no see, girl. You've grown. Where've you been, like?' He pauses then, 'I'm sorry for your loss, Lila. No one could believe it. It's not fair.'

I swallow back my tears and reach down to pet the dog. 'Thanks. I got a summer job, last year, selling ice cream and Dad was busy with the garage, so we didn't come up.'

'We missed you, didn't we?' says Connor, pulling on the rope, addressing the dog.

'I didn't know you had a dog.'

'I didn't. He's a stray, found him wandering up by the reservoir two days ago, brought him home. He's called, wait for it: Barry. Mam chose it. Bloody cissy name. I call him Baz. Mam's supposed to be bringing a proper lead home tonight.'

'Dylan's gone,' I say, 'there's no sign of him anywhere.'

'Shit! Have you tried the RSPCA? They're taking in the strays. Or the animal refuge at Moorside? He could be there. Give 'em a ring.'

'Can't get a proper signal and the phone's dead on the farm.'

'Signals are down everywhere the last day or so, nowt new there,' says Connor. 'I'll ring from home if you like, we've got a landline.'

'Thanks.'

'What you doing tonight?'

'Nothing,' I say.

'We'll be in the Black Horse, on the pool table in the back, bit of a lock-in. About eight o'clock?' says Connor. 'I'll wait for you at the bottom of the track if you like.'

'Is that allowed?' I say, 'it sounds dangerous.'

Connor shrugs. 'As long as they don't find out. There's a few of them mind, watch you like a hawk in case you dare go out more than once a day. Like Mrs. Moody, the old witch. What's it to her? Trying to close the place down, like totally. Have a heart attack if she knew half of the things that went on.'

I'm about to say I think I remember her when Baz starts barking and straining on his rope. A woman on a bicycle rides past and waves at Connor. Connor waves back, pulling Baz to heel, 'Shush, it's only Suyin,' he says. Then to me, 'She's not been here long, lives above the Chinese. It's shut though. She works in the factory with me Mam now. Nice woman, not like the old witch, Moody. Anyway, you up for it, tonight?'

'OK, I'll try,' I say and then I look at his football shirt, and I remember his first love, '*Howay the Lads.*'

'Now you're talking,' says Connor, beaming. 'Oh aye, Geordie boot boy me. Toon, through and through.' He pinches the fabric of his shirt between his thumb and first finger. 'Champion this, you need to get yourself one like it, now you're back. See you later, eh?'

When I get back to the farm Dad and Bryan are at the table eating bread with packet cheese slices and talking about borrowing a trailer from Bryan's brother up on High Riggs, to bring Mattie's sheep home.

When Bryan leaves, I say, 'Why are we getting the sheep? Who's going to look after them? I thought we were going home next week after you'd been to the solicitors and the estate agents.'

'They're all closed, as it happens, and a week or two more won't hurt will it? There's only a few Bluefaced, Arnold can't keep them forever, can barely look after his own. Anyway, it's not so bad here, is it? I mean you've seen for yourself. You've been out.'

'But I said I'd be back, and Sophie and Liam and the… and what about Dylan, Dad. Did you ask?'

'Nothing I'm afraid. Look, Sophie and Liam aren't going anywhere are they? And we'll be back soon enough, by the summer at the latest. How did you get on with Sheila's things?'

Night is different in the North. For one thing it takes a long time to get dark, and for another when it does you can see the stars, millions of them tumbling through the sky, rising above the black fells, hanging over the stone flag roofs and the heather moors. In the West, the night sky was a slate wiped clean by the amber light of the town, the flashing neon of seafront and pier. Here, it's vast.

Connor is waiting at the end of the track, his black and white striped football shirt glowing in the dusky light of a streetlamp. Does he ever take it off? Most probably sleeps in it. Baz is at his feet, still on a rope.

'Hey,' he says.

'Hey.'

'Bad news I'm afraid. It's closed, no lock-ins tonight, everyone's gone home.'

'Why,' I say, 'the police?'

'Nah, not the polis. It's Arnold, well to be more accurate, his sheep, they're out on the road some of them, the men have gone to see what's going on.'

'Fuck, some of those are Mattie's sheep. I should tell Dad.'

'Was thinking, maybe Dylan's up there at Arnold's. Stands to reason he'd follow the sheep if he could, you know, once a working dog...'

I bend to stroke Baz. 'You're right. I better go,' I say. I look up at Connor's face under the streetlight and I see it, a purple bruise stretching from his left eye half-way down his cheek. A bruise that wasn't there earlier in the day.

'Come on,' Connor says turning away quickly and pulling on the dog's rope. 'Good luck with the sheep. Hey,' he turns back, 'nearly forgot, this is for you.' He holds out a plastic carrier. 'Probably needs a wash, like.'

I open the bag and peer in at a black and white football shirt. I feel the smile spread across my face. 'Cool, thanks Connor,' I say, and because Tom has drummed it into me not to get up close with anyone, although I want to, I step back and blow him a kiss.

I hurry back up the track, clutching the shirt in its plastic bag, tight. There's something about Connor Greaves; he's kind for one thing, strong but gentle, tall like me and his smile makes me smile. As far as I know he's not on Insta and he's not the kind of person to be impressed by make-up and selfies, blowfish lips and clickbait, at least I hope not. He's probably right about Dylan. He'll be with the sheep, bound to be. I'll tell Tom about Arnold and we'll go up there and find him. I can see it clear as day, Dylan stretched out warming himself by the old man's fireplace.

I'm running now. Above me, stars make the shape of a boy and a dog chasing through the sky, willing me on. Ahead a barn owl floats silently across the night, fading at the moon. When I see Connor again, I'll ask him about that bruise.

The yard is floodlit when we pull up in Mattie's old Jeep. There are several vehicles and a group of men standing at a distance with their dogs. Arnold stands in the door in his pyjamas, an old wool coat on top. He's shaking his head as if to say what the hell's all this fuss about.

Bryan comes over to us. 'He's bloody pissed, but at least the sheep are gathered in. The sooner we move yours the better,' he says to Dad. 'No sign of the dog I'm afraid. I had a good look inside as it happens.'

Before we leave, we check the outbuildings and ask around, but no one has seen Dylan.

The stars have disappeared under a veil of ink-black cloud. There's no Dylan and Connor has a bruise like a fist on his face. As we drive back to the farm I make a list of yellow, to try and keep my spirits up: buttercup, daisy heart, mustard jar, celandine, Connor's hair, Beth's pleated skirt, custard tart, custard cream, field of rape, blackbird's beak, fish's eye, Sheila's china mug, the toecap on Bryan's boots, ragwort... Sheila battled it every year. Like her I can list its names: stinking willie, stinking nanny, cankerworm, stammerwort, dog standard.

'Best kept away from the sheep, worst of all in the dry feed. Pull it by hand to get the whole root,' said Sheila.

'Leave it for the bees,' said Mattie, 'leave it be.'

I see now that Mattie was right. The bees need all the help they can get. One in ten wild bee species is facing extinction. I read that. Without bees the world is in trouble. Come to think of it, Mattie was right about a lot of things, like how the winters are warmer with barely any snow, the summers warmer too. It wasn't surprising, he said, when they were clearing the world's forests at a rate of thirty football pitches a day. Was it a day or was it an hour or a minute? I don't quite remember.

A wild wind springs up from the east, singing through every gap in the roof, every crevice in the house, every loose frame and ill-fitting door. It whispers at my ear, the language of the North, its uneven rhythms of gust and calm unlike the silent steady rise and fall of the tide. It's barely light outside. I push down into the bed and pull the quilt up around my neck.

When the barking starts up there's no mistaking where it's coming from. I throw off the quilt and pull a jumper over Connor's old football shirt that smells of his smile and his soap. Then jeans and socks and I hurry downstairs, push my feet into a pair of wellies and run out into the yard. My heart is in my mouth. The dog is crouched down in the wind, fastened by rope to an old rusty trailer half-buried under long grass and a heap of rubber tyres. When I reach it, I see that its face is longer than Dylan's and it doesn't have that funny shaped patch of white that Dylan has over his left eye.

The People

Suyin, in hiding like a frog under stone. Hears the rain above her. She thinks of those times when she was just a kid in bed and outside the rain licking the city roofs. Her back still aches from her shift sewing in the factory. And now she's about to start again, at home. But needs must. There aren't enough scrubs to go round in the hospitals and care homes, so she's joined the volunteers. She's laid out the last of the blue fabric, pinned the pattern on top, begun the cutting out.

After Shen left, she'd tried to keep the takeaway going, one set meal a day, the menu chalked on a board outside, and collection times five minutes apart. It hadn't worked. The abuse hadn't helped. It didn't matter that she'd never set foot in China, that she was born in Soho, that her mother was white. *Fucking Chinese Bitch, Virus Spreader Get Back to Wuhan, Wuhan Slag.* Somewhere she read there was a nine hundred percent increase in hate speech, most of it on social media: #ChinaLiedPeopleDied #KungFlu.

She'd been walking just walking, her weekend daily exercise, and as a bus passed, the man coming towards her started shouting, 'Run her over. Run her over.' She crossed the road, but he followed, ran in front of her and spat in her face. For a while Suyin didn't leave home except after dark.

Madeline Potter sent a card telling her she was sorry and to please take no notice. She was welcome. They were in the same Facebook group, FortheLoveOfScrubs. Stay off Twitter they told her, mind the news. Keep sewing.

While she sews, Suyin's thoughts drift to life in the camp, with Daniel. *No to Fracking*, the placards said. She'd kept the rose, dried and papery, stuck down on a card, black with age. It was a peaceful protest. She'd carried a red rose, they all carried roses.

You could say Daniel seduced her. But you'd be wrong, the choice had been hers and she did not forget how in the camp, when it rained and the mud stuck to her shoes, he took her into the town to buy wellingtons. Her first pair. She wore them with two pairs of socks, one being his, and they were still too big.

He liked her cooking he said. Wok hot, spring onion, chilli, ginger, garlic, soy, pak choi – said he'd never had veg like it before, or fish or prawn or noodles. Mai had taught her to cook in the back of the Soho shop. Better than anything he'd ever had from a Chinese.

When it came to food he said, 'You are the queen. Do they have queens in China?'

'How do I know? I was born here,' Suyin said.

But she is still an outsider. An outsider, from the South. The family had come up in the world, out of Soho and to a new restaurant in Kent. Daniel had knocked on the restaurant door, one night after closing, when rain fell like sleet, even though it wasn't the month for it. It was water he wanted, sorry to trouble her. Dripping coat under the lamp, dark wet hair, his fringe damp on his forehead. She'd offered him tea. He'd stamped his feet and entered that wild night in June, when all was rain and a stranger at the door and nothing ever the same again.

It had taken him time to persuade her to run away with him in the van. It had taken persistence. He whispered words and kisses in her ear, he read poetry to her aloud, gave her books. Suyin came alive, a flowering in the forest of bamboo.

Now she is a ghost of herself in a strange town. Surrounded by hills. It could be worse. It might have been prison. Some of the protesters were taken and locked up. They'd got away, just in time. Then, traveller that he was, nomad born, Daniel had dropped her off, told her he had business further north, that his friend Shen would look out for her. So here she was, minding shop and Shen long gone on a North Sea ferry to Amsterdam. But it's a good cause, sewing scrubs, it's brought her out of hiding and Mr. Jarvis in the Co-op has agreed to help.

~

Coyotes on the Golden Gate Bridge, Kashmiri goats in Llandudno, the canals of Venice filled with fish; the unseen ghosts on the periphery of the world's towns and cities were making themselves known. Wild turkeys in California, sika deer in Japan in the subway stations. Last night Connor had crept down to the living room in the dark, switched on the TV, lowered the sound and watched entranced. The animals had the sense of it, the shift, the balance gone awry. When the humans move out, the animals move in. And that was all to the good.

In Connor's world animals outdid humans on every count. Dogs were loyal and good. A dog could smell your cloud scent even before you were there. They were time travellers, smelling what was to come, smelling the now and the past; who and what had travelled there. Could a dog smell the years of cowering and fear? He hoped not.

There were more dogs on the street now, more strays and even the odd sheep. Jackson said he'd seen two deer on the path by the church at dusk. The future was feral. Today was not the same as yesterday. The dogs knew, they could smell it. A tiger in the Bronx Zoo had tested positive. A lot of people were watching *Tiger King*. Connor wished he could watch it too, but they didn't have Netflix.

His heart had skipped a beat the minute he'd seen her, across the street, peering into the tea shop window. Lila was different, coming from far off, from the West. He'd known nothing but these northern hills. Some people moved on, but not Connor. The North was a place that came at you hard and cold. In the winter, the wind like a fist. Where she came from, the grass was long and lush, and dairy cattle fed on it and on the cowslips, so she said. He imagined lying in that grass, in those cowslips with Lila. She was on his mind. So was leaving, but he couldn't leave his mother to fend for herself, not at the mercy of Christian.

It was rare now for Christian to come at Connor. The balance had begun to shift, being a matter of bulk. If Connor stood between his mother and his stepfather, there was nowhere for Christian to go. But in drink Christian had the strength of ten men. He was a man possessed.

After he'd left Lila, Connor had called in at the Co-op where they were looking for people to unload deliveries and stack shelves. His mother was working extra shifts in the glove factory, making gloves for hospitals, but they still needed more money coming in. There was Baz to feed now. And besides, escaping prying eyes, getting out of the house and away from Christian had become Connor's number one priority.

The Co-op had taken one look at Connor and given him the job. He could, they estimated, do the work of two men.

'You can start tomorrow,' said Mr. Jarvis.

'Cool, thanks,' said Connor. There was of course the problem of what to do with the dog. Christian was the only one at home not working, but Christian couldn't look after a gerbil let alone a dog. He'd figure it out.

Connor spotted the twitching nets as soon as he got close. He ducked down and crawled past Mrs. Moody's window and let himself in through the back door. His mother was out at work, but he could hear Christian clashing about in the kitchen so he tiptoed upstairs and rummaged in his drawers until he found the old football shirt for Lila. He stuffed it in a plastic carrier ready for later and carried it downstairs.

The kitchen smelled of booze. Christian started up straight away, as soon as he saw Connor, ranting about the washing up not having been done and there being nothing to eat in the house. Then without warning, before Connor had said a word, he came at Connor's head with a saucepan. Baz

171

snarled and went for Christian's leg. Christian dropped the saucepan and Connor and the dog legged it out into the yard and down the back lane.

Connor hung out in the churchyard until it was time for the Black Horse to open. He needed to lie low. He'd already been reported by the Moody witch for being out and about more than once a day. He felt sick from the blow and he had a monster headache. He propped himself up behind one of the old moss-ridden gravestones and Baz put his head in Connor's lap. Connor held the plastic carrier tight in his hand. While they waited, they were joined by a robin, a ginger cat and a couple of black faced sheep.

Lila had clocked the bruise. He'd seen her eyes settle on it. She hadn't said anything and he was grateful. He didn't want to lie but it was hard to imagine telling the truth. He'd had a lifetime of making excuses.

It was dark by the time Connor got home. He put his head around the front room door. His mother was asleep in the armchair. Christian lay full stretch on the sofa. He was wearing his camouflage trousers. Connor pulled on Baz's rope and made for the stairs.

Christian shot up and went to the bottom of the stairs. 'Where the fuck've you been? You and that fucking dog. Bit me, the fucker did. If I see it in this house again it's dead. D'you hear me? Dead. Should never have brought the mangy thing home in the first place.'

Connor heard his mother attempting to pacify Christian. He closed the bedroom door and turned the key in the padlock.

~

It was all working out, at least that's what Tom thought, though he should have made the journey sooner. Lila was safe here, which is what mattered most, and truth be told he was relieved to be in the North. Once he'd got over the shock, that was. Funny thing, it didn't matter how old you were, with your parents gone and no siblings you were the child alone. The orphan. And once you'd pulled yourself out of that, death stalked. You were next, it stood to reason.

But out on the fells on the old tracks it was possible to banish death. In these ancient hills, in England's last wilderness, founded on granite, where magma rose as whinstone, a land once bathed in shallow tropical seas and river deltas, you could live forever. It had come back to him in the barely inhabited landscape, in the opening up to spring, the scent of green, the tiny mountain pansies flowering in the grass at the moor's edge. You didn't see that in the West.

Everything he'd railed against as a boy, the ugliness, the old mine workings, gritstone chimneys, quarries. Home. It pulled at his coat sleeves, sheep's wool on the wire, that old familiarity. It was in his DNA. Stitched into his being. Home wasn't where your heart was, or your head. Home was visceral, touch, sense, smell, a foot in the landscape of your childhood, a hand resting on the top of a wall, a climb that took your breath, lichen and moss, cotton grass, the first plover calling. The cuckoo in the wood.

Out on the tops, breath and space, another country, like a cloth rippling and unfurling on its way to the Borders in the North, to Lakeland, to the old coalfields of the East and the roads that dipped down to the sea. And marking it all out, closer in, were the shallow footed dry-stone walls where hares scraped their hollows for shelter; home to the small creatures, shrew and toad, stoat, wheatear, redstart, walls that lasted for centuries.

Home was in the house too: coal dust and ash, bread warming in the oven, washing drying, sheep skin, snow, summer hay meadow, quarry swimming. Ghosts everywhere. None more present than his mother Sheila. She was around,

for sure. Her words fought in his head. Her warnings –
beware the hawthorn, no flowers in the house mind, else
they'll be a death. Hawthorn bloomed in the time of plague,
drew the wolves.

And Mattie's spar box. He could swear it had eyes, like
the old man, following him around the room. Time to think
about getting rid. He'd seen others, grander in their fantasies,
in their assemblies of mineral and crystal under glass domes.
But it had mesmerised him as a boy and for a while he'd
made his own cabinet of curiosities, magpie feathers, dried
moths, fossil bones, fluorspar, a badger's skull, kept them
hidden in a shoebox under the bed.

All in all, Tom was pleased with himself. The sheep were
back in the field, the feed was sorted, the lambs checked
over, marked and ringed. He was home and it felt surprisingly
good. But as far as the dog was concerned, the one Lila had
found by the barn, the dog that she said belonged to Connor
Greaves… well it was dangerous having a dog you couldn't
vouch for around the sheep. He'd told her, no way did he
want it hanging about the place. The dog would have to go.

The Dog

When I ask about a funeral, Dad says, 'People aren't
bothering. It's not as if you can invite anyone.'

'What do you mean?' I say. 'Of course, they are. You can
have up to ten people and you can live stream it. Like Zoom.
We should have done that, why didn't we do that? Why
didn't we have a funeral?'

'We were too far away. There was no point.' Tom picks
up the plates from the table. His back is to me. Guilt and
grief hang between us.

'Well, I still think we should do something,' I say, 'even

if it's just us. Sheila wanted to be buried in the cemetery by the primroses, where you can look down on the fields and the herons nesting. You haven't forgotten, have you? And Mattie should be next to her.'

'It's too late for that,' Tom says clashing pans as he sets about the washing up.

I jump up, 'What do you mean it's too late? How can it be too late?'

'I already made the decision. I told Bryan.'

'Told him what?' I look out of the window at Sheila's garden, at the fruit bushes coming into leaf, at the leftover vegetable tops, leeks, sprouts. And the weeds. Ragwort I know, but all kinds of things are coming up that I don't recognise. All I know is the rhubarb patch and the blackcurrant bushes and the way Sheila laid nets to keep the birds off. Is it time for that? Is the garden already lost?

'I told him to go ahead for us before we got here.'

'Go ahead. With a funeral. Without us?'

'I already told you, funerals aren't what they were, Lila, you can't have people gathered like that. There was no point in waiting.'

'So, they're already there, in the cemetery,' I say doubting my own words.

'Not exactly,' says Tom.

'Not exactly, not exactly? For God's sake Dad, what do you mean?' Two brass-handled, varnished coffins make their way into my head. I watch them slip from a conveyor belt into a fiery cave to be consumed in the flames. There are no primroses, no copper leaves, no looking out to the old gravel beds where the herons nest or beyond to the goose fields. 'How could you?' I say. 'I can't believe you. How could you do that? I hate you.'

'Look...' he says, but before he can say any more, I grab my coat and make for the door.

'And that dog,' Tom shouts at my back, 'it's got to go. D'you hear me? There's no home for it here.'

Baz is waiting for me in the barn where I left him out of harm's way. I run in, kneel down and put my face in his fur. This is not how I planned it. Nothing is how I planned it. You can't make plans anymore.

Dogs are not allowed in the Co-op. I tie Baz up outside. He whines after me. He's a good dog but needy and easily spooked. He misses Connor, I know. On the door is a notice asking for donations for a woman called Suyin, who's sewing scrubs for staff in the local care homes and needs material, @suyinsews is her Instagram. I make a note to check it out. Only four are allowed in the shop at the same time.

Inside an old couple are at the freezer. The woman's hands are clutched tightly on the handle of her wire basket. I can't look. I have to turn away. It's hands that get to me, remind me. They don't show the faces of old people on the TV, not much anyway, it's mostly the hands. The papery, creased skin, the tremor, swollen fingers, thick blue veins, hands that can barely hold a spoon. They catch me out, graze my skin, crack my shell – Sheila and Mattie, how afraid they must have been and no one there to hold their hands.

~

Suyin, coat buttoned, bent, yielding like bamboo in the wind, cycling on her way to the Co-op. The scrubs on her back, packed and ready to post. She props her bicycle up outside and pets the dog tied to the lamppost. Mr. Jarvis has put the poster up, right in the centre, it hits you in the eye as you open the door. It's all there: her name and what she's doing, her Instagram. Mr. Jarvis said he'd collect donations and he's been true to his word. Only four in the shop at any one time, the notice beneath says. Suyin enters and puts her feet on the painted feet on the floor.

Mr. Jarvis beckons to the post office at the back. Suyin puts the parcels on the scales one by one.

'Postage paid,' he says and hands her fifteen pounds 74p in donations. 'There, people aren't all bad.' He smiles. Then tells her there's been a delivery of rice and flour.

There are three other people shopping, an elderly couple and a young girl. Suyin can't help but overhear the girl asking Mr. Jarvis if he's seen Connor Greaves or knows where she can find him.

'Him, that lad? Here today and gone tomorrow you mean. Gave him a job, showed him the ropes and now he decides not to turn up. Not much use if you ask me. What d'you want with him pet?'

'I've been looking after his dog, that's all,' says the girl, 'and I need to give him back.'

'Well good luck with that,' says Mr. Jarvis as he scans a ginger cake, a carton of milk and a loaf of bread.

The girl hands over a five pound note and says, 'Keep the change. Put it in the donations, for the lady making the scrubs, please.'

'Thank you pet, much appreciated.' Mr. Jarvis nods in the direction of Suyin. 'That's the lady as it happens, over there, who sews the scrubs.'

Suyin smiles at the girl, nods and mouths a 'Thank you.'

Outside the girl is about to untie the dog from the lamppost when Suyin calls to her. 'Please wait. I have a treat for the dog, if it's OK.'

The girl nods and stands back.

Suyin approaches and feeds Baz, from a small packet of dog treats. 'So, Connor, he is missing,' says Suyin. 'He's a nice boy. I hope nothing has happened. You're his friend? Do you live near him?'

'Not exactly, I'm from up on Craggs Farm.'

'Oh, I see. I am so sorry, sorry for your loss, Sheila was a kind woman.'

'Thank you,' says the girl.

'If I see Connor, who shall I say is looking for him?'

'Lila,' says the girl, 'my name is Lila.'

Suyin watches Lila go. She thinks how the birds of sorrow fly over Lila's head.

~

'It never rains here,' I say.

'Yes it does,' says Tom, 'just not as often.'

'It's dry as a bone, the earth I mean. Gardens need the rain.'

'Since when were you interested in gardens and rain? Shouldn't you be getting on with your schoolwork, Lila?'

'Whose idea was it to call me Lila anyway?'

'Beth's. It was her idea. I'm thinking of getting more sheep, of building up.'

'I miss her,' I say. It would all be so different if she was still here.

'Me too,' says Tom.

'It's not like home here,' I say, 'it's different. It doesn't feel the same. I don't know anyone, not really and...' I don't get to finish because Baz starts barking out in the barn.

'I told you to get rid of that dog,' says Tom.

'I will, just as soon as I find Connor.'

'Gone AWOL has he?'

'No. I don't know. He'll turn up.'

'He better and it better be soon because I've phoned the refuge at Moorside to come and collect it.'

I swallow hard forcing back tears, 'Why do you have to be so mean?'

'I'm not being mean, I'm just being practical.'

'Practical is mean in this case.'

'What?'

'Well, sometimes practical is good like the Chinese lady who...'

'Like, who?'

'Like the Chinese lady who lives above the takeaway, she's making scrubs for the people in the care homes. That's good. That's helping solve a problem not just getting rid of one, not just dumping a problem on someone else.'

'It's not safe to have a dog we don't know around the sheep.'

'But he's a good dog, Dad, honest, mostly he's scared. I think he's been ill-treated or something. He does as you tell him.'

'I don't care. I've made up my mind Lila the dog's got to go. They're coming in the morning.'

~

Chickens fly and dogs jump. Suyin doesn't know much about dogs but she knows it's a mess. The girl Lila nearly knocked her off her bike so she could tell it was serious. She was anxious, worried, like the tiger in the snow looking back at her footprints waiting for the hunter. Lila said the dog belonged to Connor, but she couldn't find him and now she couldn't keep him, and she begged. 'Please, please, just for a few days, until I find Connor.'

~

'Just for a few days,' I heard myself say, exactly the kind of thing Dad said to me, something you say when you're desperate and playing for time. But I couldn't let them take

Baz, could I? When the van had come trundling up the track that morning, I'd taken Baz and fled up onto the moors to the unfenced roads, snow poles, the heather that feeds the bees. To blanket bog and cattle grid. Into a world where the hills eat the sky, where you can see the earth's curve and feel it move under your feet.

You can forget the virus for a while, up here, forget that it's a symptom of all the wrong we're doing to the world. Forget the Anthropocene. You can believe in the future. High up here they say you can see the northern lights, catch a shooting star. I want to come here with Connor, show him the blue hills folding away into the distance, stretching far away to the grasses and lakes, the seas and tides, of my home.

Baz stays close, not attempting to chase the nesting grouse, as if he knows he's had a narrow escape. When we've been gone an hour or more, we venture down, off the moors onto field and track into the grey streets, in hope of what I'm not sure. The streets are empty and then suddenly she's there, the Chinese lady who sews scrubs, peddling against the wind.

I promise to bring everything the dog needs and leave it at the door of the takeaway. I don't really give her a choice just throw myself and Baz on Suyin's mercy.

~

Suyin on the sofa, the dog under the table, looking out at her. She'd forgotten to ask its name, there'd been no time and the girl Lila hadn't said, just that she was desperate. The dog had eyes on her, alert to her every move. Nervous, she thought. They were both nervous. What did she know of dogs?

Suyin fetches the packet of treats she'd bought in the Co-op and tips one into her hand. She coaxes the dog out from under the table. He's wary but can't resist and shuffles forward to meet her outstretched offering. It's a start. But how can she look after a dog? Go to work and leave it? What do dogs do all day? Where do they sleep? She'll find out soon enough. She works shifts now in the factory, odd hours, but she doesn't think that will matter much to a dog.

An upstairs flat is not ideal. In the camp the dogs had been free to run and mostly they were ignored. They nosed around the tents, hung about for scraps and Suyin fed them because nothing should go hungry and because she knew what people thought: the Chinese eat dogs. That's what they thought. And it was true, hungry people will eat what is within their grasp. She knew also that Chairman Mao had forbidden the keeping of dogs and some poor folk had been dragged into the streets to watch while their pets were beaten to death. Her father told her. But it was all in the past. It was different now, though history and reputations were hard to shake off.

Suyin is reading one of the poetry books that Daniel gave her. Do dogs like poetry? She wishes the dog would come over and sit beside her on the sofa. She's already imagining the warmth and comfort. She's imagining reading poetry aloud to it. She's never had a pet before unless you count the goldfish in the Soho takeaway, there to bring good fortune and communicate with a distant loved one, in this case her dead grandmother. When she asked why goldfish, her father told her because messages were carried in the bellies of fish and besides, he enjoyed watching them. How did the saying go? You are not fish, how would you know the happiness of fish?

Suyin supposes it is the same for dogs. She is not a dog and knows nothing of the dog's world. Daniel knew something. He was at ease with dogs. Suyin wonders where he is and if he's made his way back south on the old gypsy roads that were his home.

She gets up and goes into the kitchen. She hears the soft pad of the dog's feet as it follows her and sits under the small two-person kitchen table where there is barely room. She puts a spoonful of cold, fried mashi on a plate with a pork dumpling and slides it across the floor to the dog. He noses the plate, looks up at her and before the kettle is boiled for her tea, he's wolfed it back and is licking the plate clean.

'Ah, Chinese dog,' thinks Suyin and smiles.

May 2020

I saw the pictures on Facebook. Sophie and her family have been on a cycling trip to the dunes. We haven't spoken much, no Houseparty with Liam, no WhatsApp. I've been avoiding them, there's too much that's impossible to put into words. Mostly I send emojis, concentrate on the small things.

Dad's not expecting it when I come up behind him. He's tugging on a stem of ragwort by the path to the gate, his hands so much bigger than Sheila's.

'So, where have you put them then?' I ask.

He straightens up, turns his head, 'Lila, I didn't realise you were there. Put what?'

'The ashes. Mattie and Sheila's, where have you put them?'

'Ashes? I'm not sure, I mean, Bryan's got them, I think.'

'You think? You don't know? Bryan? Well get them back, Dad or else, or else I'll go and ask him myself. You better not be lying.'

'Don't worry, I'll get them. I'll see Bryan.'

I start to walk away.

'So, what did you do with the dog?'

'Found him a home, a loving home that's what I did, different to this. I found him a home, Dad.'

Why does it never rain in the North? I watch the weather forecast for a sign of rain. I'm not myself without it. Where are the meadows, the cows with their feet in mud and the flag irises in the streams? I think of home, I make a list: cycling the flat lanes, ditch, reed and bulrush, the tide racing in covering the mirror face of mud, swimming costume wrapped in a towel, wind blowing, boats out, storm gathering in the channel, the café by the old pier, ice cream, slot machines, fish and chips in paper on the seawall, flood tide, night fires, breaktime on the school field, blue mist, sun in a haze, skies spilling over the fields...

I remember how Beth said people were friendlier here in the North, had more time for you. It was true I could see that, but the land itself – sheep, fells, dry-stone walls, thorny gorse, stunted trees, nothing pretty or easy.

Sheep. All Dad thinks about are sheep and more sheep. I heard him tell Bryan that he feels as if he's come home. As far as I'm concerned, I might as well be on the moon.

The Quarry

The sky an insistent blue when Connor enters the quarry, the odd rag of cloud above; in the grass, primrose, dog violet, wild thyme, selfheal, the old rusted blast hut and rising above it sheer rock, gorse in flower, a single sheep on the cliff edge. What would a fall from that height mean? After the wide track a narrowing and the shadow of yew, dog's mercury underfoot, over the wooden bridge, left handrail rickety, the overhang of trees, a cleft, a cooling, an archway in the limestone, the seam of iron like blood in the rock.

The hollow is as good a place to hide as any, unseen among the grasses and tall stemmed ferns with their feathery fronds. He has his small tent and a few provisions. People walk by, walk their dogs but not in numbers. It's wild enough to escape in, to light a fire at dusk in an old tin drum.

Christian never ventures into the old quarry for fear of the gypsies camped there. No, Christian isn't about to come looking here, and anyway it's illegal to hunt with a crossbow, Christian has been warned once already by the police.

The crazy thing is they are seriously dangerous, yet any Joe Bloggs can buy one. It doesn't make sense. 175 pounds. Panther High Velocity. How cool the box looked when it came with its black and red lettering – built for power, high performance. For all the world, looking like a toy. Christian had lifted it straight out, couldn't wait, and in a matter of minutes he was pointing it at Connor and Connor had felt the heat, the familiar heat of fear rising in the pit of his guts, dragging them down to his boots. Outside in the back garden, Christian shot the bolt straight through an old telephone directory – the bulky kind. It was lethal. You could take a man's eye out; you could kill a man with a crossbow. Connor was in no doubt.

He'd tried to message Lila, just to let her know why he'd left Baz and why he wasn't going back. But he couldn't get a signal. If he could talk to Lila, he'd tell her there was no going back. That was the scariest thing of all. As to the future, he had no idea. Just that the virus and being shut up indoors had made it all so much worse. He couldn't breathe. Fear stalked, eating up every space in the house. He walked on tiptoe, on broken glass. Time for it to end, before someone got seriously hurt.

Connor was nine when Christian moved in. Six years before. A lifetime. Nine was hazy, eight, ten, eleven, twelve, likewise. The years merged indistinguishable, apart from the move from junior to secondary, Connor remembered that. He remembered certain things, moments of hope, that there might be someone to tell. But there was no clear timeline.

He remembered his seventh birthday and a cake like a train. He remembered the worst, of course he did. It haunted him.

At first small things, pinching hard, a twisted ear, a push, a slap around the head. His mother had objected at the start. Christian laughed, 'Why it's just horse play, man, it's what boys do, eh? Eh?'

Slap, kick, fist, it escalated.

And then the knife and his tricks – 'Put your hand flat on the table spread out the fingers, go on, man, hold still.' He didn't dare move for fear of the knife as Christian stabbed between his fingers, faster and faster and him praying for it to happen, to be rid of the waiting. That's when it started, he thinks. The leaving of his body, drifting up to the ceiling looking down on himself, then out beyond to the hills.

Or was it later, in the bedroom, a boy and a man in camouflage, always Christian in his camouflage. At first, he made Connor watch, but then came the touching... and it didn't stop until he asked his mother if he could put a lock on the bedroom door. He'd caught the bus into town to buy it. Still he doesn't know where he'd got the courage or why she'd agreed so readily. But once fitted that lock was the best bit of kit he'd ever owned. Ever.

There'd been no telling. Nobody had asked and who would have believed him? You can't abuse The Hulk.

Connor lies with his head on his pack. If only Baz was with him. If only he hadn't panicked and left him like that. If only Lila was here.

~

They sat a little further apart than usual, but not so you'd really notice, kept the curtains closed and the lights low. It was the custom. Stoppy backs. Most nights Albert Thomson, the local copper, and a mate of Bryan's, came in. Numbers limited themselves. Jackson refused anyone he didn't like which was no one as far as Tom could make out. Even Dodds got in. 'Shoot a thing, anything, as soon as look at it; hobby, hen harrier, he's a bloody nutter.' That was Bryan's verdict. There were those that would pay good money for the like, the keepers and such up on the moors, the fewer predators the better for the grouse and the shooting parties. Big money. It was illegal, but like most things round about there were people for and there were people against. Tom stayed neutral, he'd only just got back. It would take a while before he could reclaim his local's badge.

A coal fire flickered in the hearth. Tom sat on a wooden bench by the window, nursing his pint, waiting for Bryan. Under his feet, beneath his mud-caked boots, he felt the centuries old grey flagstones, tough and enduring, like the place. A weathered life, no cosseting. OK, so it struggled against its latitude, its cold ice-bringer winds, its stay-indoors winters – except for those who must be out on the fells after the sheep – its half-wild boys, black heather spring, mine shaft, seam and shift, fossil shells underfoot, space and breath. Here you could breathe out all right. Here there was iron in the rock.

Lila felt differently, he knew. She was angry with him and she had a right. Although she'd loved coming as a child, it wasn't her place. And he wasn't good at this grief, this talking, things a father was supposed to do. Truth be told he was barely coping himself, had to turn off the news because one thing led to another and to the image, fixed in his head, of Mattie and Sheila, alone at the end.

If it was like this for him, then what about Lila? They hadn't talked about it, not really. He'd just told her that Mattie had most likely caught it over at the Mart. He'd been warned not to go, but everyone knew Mattie was as stubborn as the day was long.

Lila had been left to soak up the loss in her own way, like she had when Beth had died. He was a crap father, too much like his own father, too spare with words, feelings buried deep. Left them all guessing, so Beth said. He wished he hadn't been so mean about the dog now, but it was too late to take it back. Though he was right, strange dogs and sheep were never a good mix.

Tom was two-thirds of the way down his pint when Bryan walked through the door. 'Another one?' Bryan mouthed.

Tom nodded.

Bryan came over, pint in each hand, put them down, soaking the beer mats.

'All right?' said Tom.

'Aye.'

'You're late.'

'It was bedlam in our house getting the bairns off to sleep and the bloody polis at the door.'

'The police what did they want?'

'House-to-house, it looks like the Greaves boy's gone missing. I'm not surprised, like, who'd want to live with that bastard.'

'What bastard?'

'That nutter Dodds, the one I told you about, kills the birds, lives with the boy's mother, Janet Greaves, has done for a canny while. Connor, they call the boy. Had a bruise like he'd been hit with a shovel over his eye and down his cheek, saw it with my own eyes. He was out with that dog of his not far from your place. I told the police, said, 'If it was me, I'd bloody well be on me bike rather than live with that pig.'

'I didn't realise,' said Tom. 'He left the dog at our place, you know.'

'Did he now?'

'Lila knows him. The dog's gone now. I told her to get rid of it because of the sheep. I didn't know about the boy,'

187

Tom shook his head, 'but it's better she's not involved by the sound of it.'

'True,' said Bryan into his pint. 'Dodds is a bastard all right, even the police are wary. Likes his crossbow too much, straight through Kevlar, they reckon.'

'Kevlar?'

'The stuff they make the stab proof vests and such out of. Can't blame the polis if they're dubious with a weapon like that on the loose. Feel sorry for the kid.'

Tom nodded in agreement and downed the rest of his pint. 'While I think of it,' he said, 'what did you do with Sheila and Mattie, the ashes I mean?'

Moths

A moth caught in a trap, that's me. Why doesn't Connor text? Moths have a lot to contend with, people should just leave them alone instead of luring them into light traps, so they flutter round and round and damage their wings.

I'm one dog down, nowhere to be seen, one on borrowed time in a foster home, and I've got a father obsessed with sheep. I have to find Connor. I've made up my mind.

Tom has other ideas.

'Here,' he says at breakfast and puts a pair of old gardening gloves on the table in front of me. 'You'll be needing these, though they might be a bit on the big side.'

'What for?' I say through a mouthful of toast.

'Gardening,' says Tom with an exaggerated enthusiasm.

'Gardening?'

'Yes, about time we spent some time together, thought we could dig over the garden, you know turn it over, weed it, maybe even plant a few veg. All this fine weather has got everything sprouting.'

I look out onto Sheila's garden, abandoned, unloved, it would have broken her heart to see it like this. I hesitate, what about Connor? I was going to look for Connor, but I can't tell Tom that, 'But... it'll just go wild again, when we leave, won't it? So, what's the point?'

'Come on, you don't mean that,' says Tom. 'You were always out there with Sheila. You know better than me what needs doing. Besides...'

'Besides what?'

'I thought we could scatter the ashes there, Sheila loved it and Mattie too, liked to sit out on that little patch of grass on a Sunday in the summer.'

'Have you got the ashes, then?' I say, looking down at the gloves on the table.

'Bryan's got them, keeping them safe for when we're ready. What do you say we make a start, the weather's perfect?'

Out together, sun on our backs, clearing brambles and nettles. Sheila is in the garden with us. Sheila is guiding me. Now I see the plants up close I realise I know the names of most things. I realise what she taught me.

Tom is forking over the veg patch, unearthing last year's leavings. I'm teasing the weeds from the wide border where the foxgloves will flower and the ox-eye daisies, the lavender and old roses. In the shade of the low stone wall, by the gate, yellow poppies and lady's mantle are already up. We clear the fruit trees and Tom mows the small patch of lawn. On the path a song thrush waits, eyeing the worms.

I fetch lunch, a tray with cheese and pickle sandwiches, mugs of tea and a packet of Jaffa cakes. We sit to rest and admire our handiwork. Above us lapwings waver and call in the cloudless blue.

It's official, skies are bluer, the bluest they've been for decades, due to the absence of pollution. There are things to celebrate, there is change to come. But for now, as I sip my tea, a feeling of unease flutters in my chest like a small, trapped bird. I'm thinking of Connor. He would never leave Baz unless it was serious, I know that much.

I make a list of blue to calm: a plastic free ocean, harebell in the grass, larkspur, the taste of morning, a sapphire ring, shadow of my mother's arm around me, smoke in the trees, bird's egg, mussel shell, Connor's eyes, at least I think they're blue, Mattie's old jacket that Tom's wearing now...

For an hour or so after lunch we work in silent harmony and I can't remember the last time, if ever, that we spent this much time together, apart from in the car. I take off the gloves, I want to feel the earth under my fingers, I don't mind the scratches or the dirt.

You can bury a lot of troubles digging in the garden, it comes to me in Sheila's voice, quickly followed by, *ne'er cast a clout 'til May be out*.

'It's too early for planting,' I say to Tom as he stands to survey the veg patch. 'But when we do, we need to think of the bees. And a tree, we should definitely plant a tree.' Trees are our lungs. Just one tree is home to hundreds; insect, lichen, mammal, plant. We need more in the world not less.

'Agreed,' says Tom. 'But enough for now, we need to clean up. And I'm going to make us spag bol for tonight.'

I leave the curtains open, moonlight flocks the room, turning solid to liquid, wood to starlight. The white stripes of my football shirt gleam. Moths flutter at the glass. I turn the bedside lamp off to quiet them. I'm propped up in bed, the table of tides safely tucked under my pillow, scrolling through my phone. Sophie's got a boyfriend and so has Liam, they met on MyLOL, I should check it out Sophie says.

Nothing from Connor.

He can't be that far away. He's hiding somewhere, I'm sure

of it. I'll start my search tomorrow. I pick up my notebook and pen lying on the quilt next to me and make a list of places to hide: the ruined farmhouse on the way to Arnold's, the sheep pens on the moors, the old barn where the owls nest, the entrance to the drift mine, the alder wood, the river, the quarry, the churchyard and everywhere in between...

I put down the pen. My arms and my back ache from the day's work but I'm happy we've brought the garden back to life. If only Dylan was here. I worry about Suyin and the dog, I should DM her. I worry about the world and the trees being cut down, I checked up on what Mattie said, it's thirty football pitches a minute, not a day. I can hardly believe it. I don't want to believe it. I'm tired, I pull the quilt up and burrow into the pillow somewhere between awake and sleep...

...Sheila is here, hands soft but gritty, like sand on the shore, smoothing my hair, kissing me goodnight, telling me not to worry. Sheila who smells of lavender, who drinks her tea green because it's good for you, who eats tinned peaches with evaporated milk, who plants when the moon is waxing. Sheila, who is not the kind of woman to take her own life.

It was Mattie who fell ill, though according to Tom, no one seemed to know, not even the doctor. He was stubborn, independent as the day was long, it had always been his way. Some people know when their time has come and they're ready for it, Tom said. The postman found them. Sheila had climbed into bed next to Mattie, an empty bottle of tablets lay beside her on the quilt. The curtains were left open. I like to think she left them for the moon to look in, for the silent papery winged moths to gather on the sill.

Above me the distant drone of a helicopter circling the fields.

~

The moon like a lotus in a dark pool, the dog asleep at the foot of Suyin's bed – the long thoughtfulness of the night lying ahead. Moonlight transforms. The camp looked different under the moon, dirt and stone were as silk, and the possibilities of night stretched out on its lit path. It was her favourite time in the camp, while others were sleeping, she stole the night for herself. The pale green light, the absence of sound, of clatter or voice, would draw her up out of her sleeping bag to walk along the footpath, to lose herself in the wood among the shadow of trees.

The dog stirs and snuffles, then settles back into spot on the bed. They are growing used to each other. Tomorrow she will take him for a long walk among trees, by the river. To the quarry she thinks, let him explore to his heart's content, maybe even swim in the river. Do dogs swim?

Suyin thinks of the boy. A worried dog can jump over a wall. All day Janet Greaves' machine had lain idle, her seat empty. Gossip flourished. Suyin learned the suspicions of the women. The police had come to question them one by one. For some reason she omitted to tell them she was looking after Connor's dog.

Above her a helicopter like an approaching storm, its thudding call like a warning, longer, louder. Moths hide, sheep huddle, squirrels are blown from their nests, then for a moment the beam of its searchlight overhead flashes into the room, drowning out the moon. When the helicopter turns away and its thunder fades, Suyin leaves a message with the moon to watch over the boy, wherever he is, and to watch over Lila too.

~

Some dreams are hard to shake off, like walking into an unseen web, its fine skeins sticking to your skin. Tom had been out in a blizzard with Mattie, snow driving at them from the north. They were digging out a ewe and her lamb, but no sooner did they uncover them than the snow piled up around them again. It was impossible to dig fast enough. Dylan was there with them, barking and running around in circles. Then Sheila, arms outstretched emerged like a spirit from a white wall of snow, calling his name.

He woke then, made himself sit up, not wanting to fall back into the dream. Regret stalked. He should have moved up to help them long before, after Beth died, he should have come back then. He would have been here to shield them, to be the son they deserved. Tom swung his legs out of bed and went out onto the landing. Lila's door was ajar. He went to close it, softly, to make sure not to wake her. He peered in but there was no Lila to wake. The covers were pulled back and the bed was empty. Lying open on the quilt was a notebook. Tom picked it up and read a list of places in Lila's handwriting, one underlined, it wasn't hard to imagine why. He threw the notebook back on the bed and ran downstairs calling her name, then out into the yard. But Lila was nowhere to be seen.

Ferns

Bird song. A dawn chorus, the blackbird sweetest and loudest, heralding the day. Connor stirs from sleep, remembers where he is. He is here, in the woods, safe, no heart sink, no pit of fear threatening to swallow him as he wakes. He drifts back into dream until the first rays of light fall on the tent.

The helicopter had come close, but the trees had shielded him. He stretches and works his way out of the sleeping bag. His back aches. Sleep had been impossible and that would have been all right if he'd been at home on the old laptop. Most of his friends stayed up online through the night like vampires. After all, there was nothing much to get up for. But he'd been alone, hungry and cold.

Now morning has come and he has to move on before they find him and send him home and the whole merry-go-round starts again, trapped in the house with a monster. No escape. Even here in the safe place, the monster lives in his head. It feeds on his thoughts, creeps up on him when he's least expecting it, inhabits him, sends him careering up, out of his own body, to look down on someone he barely knows.

All he can think is to get as far away as possible. He must pack up and go, but first he must see Lila and explain. He's made up his mind. He can't leave without seeing Lila and he can't leave without Baz. He can't be alone. Connor unzips the tent and pokes his head out. The sky is cloudless, the world made over, washed clean. If only that were possible for him.

~

I woke suddenly, in the grey light before the dawn. The moths had gone. It came to me in a dream, that's how it seemed. I knew where Connor was. Of course I did. I didn't need the list. I knew where to find him.

That summer, two years ago; making a rope swing across the river where the flat stones made a pavement, plodging in the shallows, drying off and sunning ourselves among the ferns in the hollow, then hiking along river to the common where the rocks opened out and the day trippers picnicked and we bought ice pops from the ice cream van. We'd spent all our time in the quarry.

In the half-dark, half-light I hear the call of a cuckoo. The air is cool, it's damp underfoot and the quarry smells of morning. I pass the pool where shadowy grey fish lurk under frogbit, and hurry to the old wooden bridge. I cross it, careful not to slip, then through the cleft in the rocks and along to the hollow. Then I see it, a little way ahead, a small green tent, easily missed, but it's there all right and now whoever is inside is unzipping it. A head and shoulders poke out. I'd know that head and that football shirt anywhere.

~

Connor is out of the tent, standing up, looking out through the gauze of overhanging leaves. It's her. Lila. He'd know that football shirt anywhere. It can't be. But it is. Connor's heart bangs in his chest. He whistles long and low and Lila raises an arm and waves. Now here she is, coming through the grass and the dew-lit ferns into the hollow.

She's the first to speak, breathless with hurrying, 'Connor, I knew I'd find you here.'

'Lila.'

She stops, a few feet in front of him, an awkward pause, then he says, 'Here. Sit here,' and points to a boulder in the grass. Lila sits. Connor goes inside the tent and fetches a towel. 'Here you'll be wet walking through that lot.'

She wipes her jeans, 'Thanks,' and hands him the towel.

He throws it back in the tent and then comes and sits on the boulder beside her. 'How did you know where to find me?'

'That summer, we spent all our time here, with Maeve and Jo-jo. Maeve called it "our happy place," didn't she? So, I guessed it's where you'd be.'

'Yeh, she did, that's right.' Connor smiles and they are quiet for a moment as if both recalling the time spent together. Then he says, 'I was wondering about Baz. I'm sorry I left him like that. I didn't know what else to do. I thought, if I took him with me, he'd bark and stuff and then they'd find me.'

'He's good,' says Lila. 'I just couldn't keep him. I'm sorry, but Dad wouldn't allow it, said he couldn't have a strange dog around the sheep, so I asked the Chinese lady.'

'Suyin?'

'Yes, Suyin. She's got him. For a few days anyway. I was hoping you'd be back. He'll be missing you. You are coming back, Connor, aren't you?'

Connor sighs, 'I don't think so, I'm sorry but I just can't.'

'But why not? Where will you go? They've been looking for you. I think they've had the police helicopter out.'

'I know, I heard it last night when I was lying in the tent, praying they wouldn't catch me with that infrared thing. Couldn't sleep. It was freezing. Don't know, don't know where I'm going, Lila, but I can't go home.' Connor's shoulders slump he puts his head in his hands. 'It's Christian, my stepdad. I can't go back and live with him. I'd rather die. Don't know what I'm gonna do.'

'Is that where the bruise came from?'

Connor lifts his head. 'Yes.'

~

I feel angry and sad at the same time. The thought of it, of someone hurting Connor like that. As always, I swallow my tears. I'm used to it. I mustn't cry. If I'm not careful I'll start and there'll be no stopping me. That's the danger. I'll cry for all of us, for Connor, for myself, Beth, Mattie and Sheila. I'll cry for the world and everyone in it and what we've had to endure. There's no time to make a list, so I reach out and take Connor's hand, so much bigger than mine. 'I'm sorry,' I say as I let a single tear fall.

Connor leans towards me. 'Don't cry, Lila, please.' He

keeps my hand in his, my heart is racing from the touch of him, with his other hand he pulls a crumpled tissue from his pocket and wipes my cheek. 'There,' he smiles. His eyes meet mine. He reaches his hand up to touch my face and then there is no distance between us. Connor's lips are on mine. Cool and soft. It feels forbidden. Our kiss tastes of canvas and ferns and peanut butter. And I don't want it to stop.

When we come up for air, he's still holding my hand.

He runs his fingers along the scratches, 'What have you been up to?' he says, lifting my hand to his mouth and kissing it.

I'm not expecting it. The kiss on my hand. The tenderness. It's hard to speak when someone is kissing you like that. I have to wait until he finishes. Then I say, 'Gardening, yesterday with Dad, we were just trying to sort the garden out before it got lost in weeds, get it ready for planting, like Sheila did.'

A smile, wide as a river spreads across Connor's face. 'Aye, just like my Granda, on his allotment, every year. I used to love it there, never minded helping him weed. Loved it even when it rained, then we'd sit in the shed and he'd make a brew. Grew leeks like soldiers, canny fat ones, flowers for the bees, comfrey for compost. Never forgot the wildlife. Loved it all, birds, bees, hedgehogs, bats you name it. Wouldn't hurt a fly.'

'We're going to scatter Sheila and Mattie's ashes in the garden.'

'Sounds like a cool thing to do. I wished we'd done that for my Granda.'

'I'll have to go soon,' I say. 'Dad will be awake and he'll realise I'm gone. I'll come back though. Later. I can bring Baz if you like.'

'Stay for a bit,' says Connor. 'Half an hour won't make

any difference. Let's go inside. I've got a peanut butter sandwich left.'

We go inside, share Connor's last sandwich then lie back on the sleeping bag. Before long we are in each other's arms. Before long Connor is asleep, and I wish I could stay forever in this safe, green bubble of home. I don't remember ever being as happy as I am now. If only Connor would stay. If only I could help him. If only I could persuade him.

I make a list and whisper it into the air around us, reasons for Connor to stay: me and you, lead and silver, black cockle, beck and burn, a poet's world – a Never Never Land of dreams, Mattie taught me that – butterburr and bee, forest and lea, Newcastle United football club, over the ford, stepping stones, Jo-jo and Maeve – they must be around somewhere, can't be too far away – nothing above you but sky, cloud shadows racing across the fells, hives and bell heather, wavy grass and sorrel, the robin in the churchyard, saving what is lost, together, belonging and Baz, Lila… stay for me.

~

Sun replaces moon. Suyin is up early to let the dog out into the yard. Then breakfast: more mashi for him with a bowl of dried dog food, tea for her. He follows her from room to room. A dog with separation anxiety she thinks. A dog not entirely at home; stranger in a strange landscape she knows how he feels.

She sits at the table and drinks jasmine tea, eats rice porridge and honey. The dog sits on her feet. She orders the next batch of fabric for scrubs. The sewing must not be forgotten. There is a need.

And there's plenty of time before her two o'clock shift for a walk in the quarry. Suyin puts on her shoes and coat and sets out with Baz obedient at her feet. A blue-sky day, sun rising, spring moving into summer, the ripe downy seeds of catkin on the breeze, fledgling sparrows, cow parsley and the trees looking pleased with themselves, coming into full leaf. It was all lying here in wait she thinks, beneath the winter snow, soundless and deep.

On mornings such as these she has no regret in landing here: this one wild place, this secret kept, space and breath, wide green vista. Green has become Suyin's favourite colour in its numberless shades: the smallest of seeds breaking through, the hills near and far, yew green in the churchyard darkening to black, the glaucous leaf of eucalyptus, the purple-green of fog grass, silver of carnation leaf, the scent of green – wildflower, rain and sun.

Suyin is downhill, approaching the quarry when she hears the first siren. A blue light flashes by. Baz is skittish, jumpy as a nervous horse. Ahead at the entrance there are more lights, more police cars, two, no three. She hesitates, pulls Baz to heel so that they blend into the trees. She keeps her distance, watches, sees them coming out of the quarry, first the dark uniforms, then the boy Connor, and with him Lila.

Someone not in uniform is reaching out to Lila, her father perhaps. He puts his arms around her. The small hunched figure of Janet Greaves steps out of a police car. She puts out a hand and touches her son on the arm.

Lila and Connor are safe. Her message reached the moon. Suyin turns and walks home.

On the two o'clock shift, all the talk is of finding Connor. It was a tip-off. An early morning dog walker spotted his tent. According to Susie Banks, who is Janet's best friend and sits on the machine next to hers, it was all Christian's fault. He'd been making Connor's life a misery, Janet's as well, and she'd had enough, told him to get out. Shoved his things into black bin bags and thrown them onto the grass.

Told him never to come back. She's taking an injunction out. Connor is fine. The boy is safe at home getting on with his schoolwork.

Can a boy really be fine, alone in the house with his schoolwork, after all of this? Suyin wonders. How much is he missing Baz? And how long before she and her little Chinese dog are parted?

~

Tom was on his way to the quarry when his phone rang. It was Bryan with news from Albert, the copper who drank in the Black Horse. The boy had been spotted there and a girl who looked like Lila with him. The relief, a long exhalation of breath, his shoulders slumped, it made sense, it was what he'd prayed for.

Mountain Pansies

Dad is making pancakes for breakfast.

'I think we should see about getting the dog back,' he says as he serves up the first pancake, lemon wedges on the side, sugar on the table.

I look up from my pancake, 'Really? I'll message Suyin, go and collect him later.'

'We can go together,' says Tom. 'We'll drive down.' He sits down with his pancake and spoons sugar into its middle, followed by a good squeeze of lemon. 'Not bad, eh?' He says after the first mouthful. 'Just like Sheila made.'

'I think Connor will want him back, if he's staying, at home I mean.'

'I told you what Bryan said, the Dodds fella's gone, thrown out. Connor'll be safe now. Just needs to behave himself, stay indoors, get back to some schoolwork, like you, I might add.' Tom smiles.

'OK I get the message, but it doesn't mean we can't meet up does it? You're allowed, you can meet up to six people as long as you're outside. Friends, I mean.'

Tom can't know we're more than friends. When he'd asked me on the way back, why, and what we were doing in the tent together, I said, 'Just talking.' I mumbled something about Connor and how badly he'd been treated by Christian, how he needed all the friends he could get. Tom seemed happy with that. And it was true, and I was allowed to keep some things to myself, wasn't I? You didn't have to tell your father everything.

'More pancakes, Dad?' I say.

'Wouldn't say no.'

I go to the stove and put the frying pan back on the heat, stir the pancake mixture. 'Just enough left for two.'

'I thought, after this, we could finish up in the garden. Bryan's going to drop the ashes off later. We could scatter them. What do you think?'

'I think that's a great idea,' I say yawning.

'Maybe go back to bed first for an hour or so? It's still early,' says Tom.

'OK, just an hour.'

I lie on the bed, wrapping myself in the quilt. I'm back with Connor in the sunlit green of the tent, reliving those first kisses. His arms are around me, pulling me close. Maybe this is home after all, I think, as I drift into the glass lantern slide of dreams.

The afternoon is fine, unseasonably so. I try not to worry about the warming, the waters rising and the cities sinking, instead I'm grateful for the sun like a gift that makes up for the hardship and isolation that people are suffering.

By the time we finish planting out the beans and sweet peas – plants left by neighbours we have yet to meet – the sun is falling in the sky, touching the hills and fields; rose, copper, gold, catching the yellow lichen and the spider's web on the dry-stone wall and beneath them the folded wings of a hawkmoth.

We don't pray, or sing, or speak. We don't do any of the things people normally do at such times. Times are different. We each take our handful of ashes, hold them up and scatter them gently into the coming dusk and its accompanying breeze. Mattie and Sheila are lifted up to fly among the crescent wings of the swifts that circle the eaves.

~

Connor lay in bed, next to him on the bedside table were sandwiches and a flask.

'Don't bother getting up,' his mother said. 'Don't worry, you're safe now. No need for this,' she had the padlock in her hand. 'He's gone for good. Tomorrow we'll see about getting that dog back. I'm popping out now, just groceries. I'll lock you in. Who was that girl by the way, in the tent with you? Was that her father, I knew him from school, at least I think I did. Tom, something? Craggs Farm. They're dead aren't they? A real tragedy that. Your football shirt's washed and drying on the line, it's a fine day for it. Back soon.' She kissed his head.

After she left and he heard the key turn in the lock, Connor put his phone on to charge and sent Lila a *Miss U* text. He wanted to say more, much more. He wanted to say *ILY* with a red heart, *ILYSM* but maybe that was over the top and besides when he says it, he wants it to be in person. It means too much. He wants her to stay here in the North. Forget the West, he wants to say, this is home now. He texts again, *U OK?* He hopes she's not in trouble. He'll text her later about Baz.

If only he could get Baz back. Now. He's still on high alert, listening for every sound in the house, every voice floating in from outside. He's not falling for it – that it's all over. Just like that. Christian gone. He knows him and he knows his mother. It's happened before. Christian worms his way back in with the sorrys he doesn't mean and she forgives him. And in no time the fists come out and the silence and the secrets start up.

He can't afford to let his guard down. He still needs a plan and for that he needs to stay strong and whole. No letting the ragged strands of him loose, no ending up crouched in the corner of the ceiling. No giving in to feeding the monster. When he's with Lila, Connor feels whole. He knows it's possible. But this trust thing, the thing he has with her, is leaky, breaks off, morphs into suspicion and paranoia. Can he be safe? Can it be safe to stay? Is it over? Ever?

~

'It's our last morning together, little dog,' Suyin says. She's always called him dog never Baz, and little, even though he's a good size, and it's too late to change now. 'They're coming for you at eleven.' She's gathered his things and packed him some pork dumplings. They've been out for a last long walk together to the elephant trees. 'I'll miss you, dog,' she says as she sips her tea. Baz sits at her feet looking up at her, as if he understands. Maybe she'll get a dog of her own, a rescue dog in need of a good home. She hopes the material will arrive soon so she can start sewing again.

Madeline Potter has invited her to tea in the garden, bring your own flask. She is thinking of forming a community group, of making something good out of this. People will still need their help. Madeline is a good person. Suyin is reminded of something her father said – when the winds of change blow, some people build walls and others build windmills. Madeline is a builder of windmills.

~

Suyin had seemed sad and faraway, as if she was trapped behind glass. I know how that feels, I knows what lives behind glass. On the way home I make a list: sorrow, loss, the two-headed calf, Mattie's spar box, other people's houses, a red anatomical heart, a leafless tree of birds, a sparrow's nest, shell and clock, plants that survive the dark, rain, fir cone, trapped bee, fly, dying moth.

It's easy to love a dog and hard to give a dog up. And who knows what the dog wants? I think of Dylan, how I've given up looking for him, or ever expecting to find him. Is it a bad thing? To give up so easily. Soon Baz will be back where he belongs. I'm meeting Connor tonight at the bottom of the track.

'After dark? Is that a good idea?' Tom asks.

'It's Connor, he doesn't want people to see him, Dad, like old Mrs. Moody for one, she'd most likely phone the police, even though it's allowed now. He just feels safer in the dark.'

'OK but take your phone, just in case, and answer it, no voicemail and no more than an hour or I'll be down there myself. Promise?'

'I promise.'

I can see him, in the shadows at the end of the track, half in and out of the old streetlight. He's wearing his football shirt. Baz is already straining at the lead. I let him off and he races to Connor, barking, tail wagging like mad, in that kind of dog ecstasy that reminds me of Dylan.

Then Connor's arms are around me, pulling me in, the dog between our feet. Connor is clinging fast, pulling me into the shadows. I smell the night around us, the earth giving up its moisture, the moss, the May blossom and the damp stone walls. I smell Connor, his soap, his football shirt.

'You OK?' I say, when he loosens his grip.

'I am now. Cool. And you?'

'I'm OK but I haven't got long. Baz is pleased to see you.' I hand over a carrier with Baz's food. 'What are you going to do, now?' I ask, praying he will say he's staying. That everything's OK. That he's not going to run away again.

'I'm not sure,' says Connor, 'I want to stay but...'

'But he's gone, isn't he, Christian?'

'For now, but who knows. Guys like him, they don't give up easily. I've seen it before. It's over. Finished. Then before you know it, a few weeks later and he wheedles his way back in and he's sorry and he's going to be good, so good this time and it won't happen again. I've heard it all before.'

'But if he comes back can't you go to the police?'

'Not if she lets him in. She says she won't, says it's different this time, but I don't know. She's keeping the door locked, so that's cool. I have to go, she's waiting, didn't want me to come out.'

'Me too. Dad's on the prowl. Could meet you tomorrow outside the Co-op. I can go down for bread, you could be walking Baz. That way I'll see you and I'll know you're OK. Then maybe you could come to ours, in the garden, in a day or so. I'll ask my dad.'

'OK. Cool. Ten o'clock?' He kisses me and buries his face in my hair. He says, 'I love the way your hair smells. Now I'll smell it on my pillow. Sleep tight. See you tomorrow. Come on, dog, let's go home.'

I watch him go, past the churchyard and out of sight, then make my way back up the track to the farm, the green tree of him blossoming in my heart.

~

Mrs. Moody's house is in darkness, no need to creep past. As he approaches the house, Connor sees the kitchen light is on. She'll be making tea. They'll sit and drink tea and eat biscuits and watch some TV. Or toast. He could eat a mountain of toast. Just one night under canvas and he could eat a horse. What he would have done after two or three nights is anybody's guess. Hunger would have smoked him out for sure. He puts his hand over the back gate and feels for the latch. He lifts it up and pushes the gate open with his foot, into the backyard. He ducks under the washing line and pulls Baz away from nosing the bins. He takes his key out turns it in the lock, but the door is open. She must have forgotten to lock it behind him. He calls out 'Hi, I'm back.'

~

Tom is waiting for Lila, watching from the window, leaving the door open, going outside into the garden, looking out to the track. When he sees her coming he breathes out. She's been less than an hour and he's grateful for that. Later when she's safe in bed he'll pour himself a drop of Mattie's whisky and dare to think about the future. Going back might be best for Lila, though he has little appetite for it. The future for him is here in the farm but not if it means Lila suffers. He has to be careful, more than before. He's not sure about Connor. The boy seems nice enough, a good kid by all accounts, but she's too young to get mixed up in his kind

206

of trouble. But the farm, he could make the farm work, he's sure of that. When things get back to normal, diversify, specialise. He'll have to talk it through with Lila. Perhaps she's growing used to the place after all. She seems to like Suyin and they know her at the Co-op. Perhaps they should get a dog. As Lila comes in through the gate into the garden Tom is waiting in the open door.

~

As soon as she comes off shift, Suyin puts a pizza in the oven and is ready in no time to begin. There isn't time to think of the dog, or what's missing. The table is spread with blue fabric, the pattern pinned and tacked. Suyin leans over, scissors in hand, guiding the blades, following the tissue edge, as she cuts. The sound of the blades as calming as a steady rain.

Madeline has been on Instagram showing off her latest sets, encouraging them. They are on their way to two hundred, another milestone. Suyin knows sewing is good, not just because the scrubs are badly needed but because it diverts, from the news, from the ever-increasing death toll. Sewing absorbs and it's something she can do. She's not alone, people are looking to help, some even trying to sign up at the factory.

When she came to collect the dog, Lila said she'd like to learn, though she didn't have a sewing machine. Suyin offered to help, they could find a spare machine no problem. She would show Lila, once the rules were relaxed and they weren't reduced to standing two metres apart in the yard. She could make masks, Suyin suggested, they might be needed, it would be a good start.

She'd handed over the dog with some dumplings wrapped in foil in a plastic bag and one of the poetry books Daniel had given her. For a moment the dog had seemed reluctant to go. She missed him, as she knew she would, she missed him sitting on her feet while she sewed and ate, following her from room to room, keeping her company through the night.

She'd liked Tom, that was his name. He'd seemed friendly and he'd been complimentary about her efforts on behalf of the care homes, said the most he'd done was clap on Thursdays and no one could hear that, all the way up on Craggs Farm. He'd thanked her for looking after the dog. Perhaps Tom and Lila were like Daniel, the people you were destined to meet, connected to you by an invisible thread.

~

The kitchen smelled of booze and fear. On the floor by Connor's feet was Christian's overnight bag. From it spilled a pair of trainers, a black hoodie, and his crossbow, primed with a bolt. Christian was standing behind Connor's mother a manic grin on his face and a knife in his left hand. His right arm was wrapped around her neck, pressing on her throat.

Her eyes were wide with fear. Her eyes said, go back, Connor, go back out of the door. Now. Go get help.

But he couldn't leave her and besides his legs had turned to jelly. He hoped Christian couldn't see. He willed himself to stand fast. His heart was in his mouth. Baz began to bark. Connor tightened the leash.

'So, the boy's back, come back to Mummy, eh?' Christian loosened his grip on Connor's mother and shoved her away from him, hard, into the sink side. She doubled over and fell to the floor. Christian held on to the knife. 'Come on then, big boy, fancy it? Come on gay boy, little shit. You and the dog. I'll take you both.' He was swaying, slurring his words.

Connor looked down at the crumpled figure of his mother. Rage rose in him like a fire from the pit of his stomach to his head until he felt he might explode. His anger was a coat with its tails lifted, streaming out behind him and before he knew it, he'd let go of Baz, snatched the crossbow and bolt from the bag, put it to his shoulder and fired.

~

I can't put my phone down. I check constantly but still there's no message from Connor. A fierce wind has sprung up, laying waste to spring gardens. Blossom is torn from trees. The leaves turn their backs to silver as I make my way down the track to the Co-op.

It's ten twenty-five when I get there. I peer in at the window, but no sign of him. I wait outside, huddled into the stone. When I've been waiting twenty minutes or more and there's still no message and I'm thinking of giving up, Mr. Jarvis comes out.

'You OK, pet? Do you need something?'

'I'm waiting for a friend,' I say.

'Would that be Connor?'

'Yes, that's right.'

'I think you better come inside, pet,' says Mr. Jarvis. As he opens the door to usher me in, Suyin appears, looking as if she might be blown off her bike, and then Dad, hurrying down the street, calling out.

'Lila, Lila.' He arrives out of breath.

Suyin pulls up and gets off her bike.

'What is it? What's happened?' I say, looking from one to another. They are standing in a ring around me, Mr. Jarvis, Dad, Suyin.

'It's Connor,' says Tom.

'I think we should go inside,' says Mr. Jarvis. We follow

him in and he turns the sign on the door from open to closed.

~

The Co-op manager, Tom didn't know his name, had ushered them into the storeroom, found chairs and made them tea. There had been no easy way to tell her, so he'd told her straight, there in the back of the store. He'd had it from Bryan, who had it from the horse's mouth: Dodds had forced his way into the house, held Connor's mother at knifepoint and Connor had shot him with the crossbow. Dodds was critical in hospital and Connor was in custody.

~

July 2020

Suyin makes her way up the track to the farm. The hedges are blowsy with summer, lined with rosebay, mallow and wild honeysuckle. In the fields they are turning the hay. Above her swallows feed on the wing. She goes through the gate into the garden where the sweet peas and roses are in bloom and the beans are tall and laden with pods. There is a newly planted tree in the border. Tom and Lila stand waiting in the doorway and at their feet sits Baz.

Lila looks different now, older she thinks. She had the worst of it, after the boy. It was only natural she would suffer. The death of the heart is the saddest thing, but Suyin knows Lila is young and still has far to go. She is teaching her to sew. Now it's possible to be in the house, they sit together and sew in Suyin's upstairs flat. Some evenings they sew at the farm. Tom has bought Lila a second-hand sewing machine.

Suyin had got it all planned. So she thought. In the Ghost Month she would light a lotus lantern and set it away downriver to guide Christian Dodds' soul. She would offer food and drink for he was not likely to have been fed or if he had, he would not have swallowed due to his needle-thin ghost neck. He would surely have suffered. He would be wandering homeless. She would not let the ghost of Christian Dodds intrude or bring misfortune, more than he had in life.

But in the end, it had not been necessary. By some miracle Christian Dodds had survived. According to Madeline he was recovered and out shooting birds again, though as likely as not to miss. He was not the man he once was and there were many who gave thanks for that.

At least the boy did not have to fear him. In the factory they agreed that it had been a good thing, Connor going to Australia, taken in by his mother's cousin. It was a long way for certain, but a new start. His mother Janet was planning on joining him, so she said. Suyin wasn't so sure. To be so far from home so young, would be like swallowing the wind, the feet may leave but what about the heart?

~

I couldn't have known what the year would hold. How I would leave home and come to the North. How I would meet Connor. And how when they sent him away, to the other side of the world to start again, it would break my heart.

He was not to blame but I was sure that no matter how far he went, he would take the guilt with him. How must it feel, knowing that you'd harmed someone, that he might have died? Do you pray to be forgiven, to forget? To me the miles were like snow on the winter fells. It made no

211

difference how long and deep, someday the thaw would set in, someday the frozen carcass of the ewe caught in the storm's drift would surface. Some things you could not escape.

More than anything I wanted him to know it wasn't his fault. I longed to put my arms around him and comfort him, but I didn't get the chance. It all happened so quickly. He was locked away, no phone, then before I knew it he'd been released, Christian had dropped all charges, and Connor was gone. I wrote him a letter and sent a poem, *A House Called Tomorrow* by Alberto Ríos. I copied it out, from the book Suyin gave me – *You are not fifteen, or twelve, or seventeen ... You are a hundred wild centuries... Everyone who has come before you, All the yous...*

I hoped it would make him feel better. I hoped it would remind him of me. I wanted him to believe in tomorrow, to know that the bad do not win – not finally, no matter how loud they are. I wanted to believe it too.

I'm waiting to hear.

It is a warm, windless afternoon, crackling with bees and smelling of new mown hay and wild thyme, when I go walking with Suyin, Baz at our heels, high up in the Dale where the mountain pansies grow. We walk in a shimmering carpet of violet and yellow, among the small, fragile faces that hover above the grass, silently mouthing their resilience. Here in the North, the mountain pansies survive no matter what. Suyin says pansies are for thoughts. They are called heartsease, and they will heal a broken heart.

Acknowledgements

My thanks as always to Lynn Michell for her generous and astute editing and her bravery and determination in keeping a small press alive in such challenging times. Thank you to my writing buddy, Wendy Robertson, for her inspiration and for our writing conversations, and to Gillian Wales for her enduring support. A special thank you to my dear friend, Marney Harris, for casting her naturalist's eye over *this One Wild Place*. Likewise to Sarah Cassidy for giving the text her eagle-eyed attention. Any errors are entirely mine. Thank you to the lovely Linen Press interns, Chania Fox, Emma McKay and Aisling Jackson Cousin. Special thanks to Chris and Susan for the mountain pansies, and to John, as always, for being my first reader.

Lightning Source UK Ltd.
Milton Keynes UK
UKHW022156070622
404067UK00008BC/2044